MW00973508

Blackbird

A Stepbrother Romance

by Abigail Graham

Chapter One

Victor

I live in studio apartment over a massage parlor in the Old City. It's a six block walk to the liberty bell. It's two flights of wrought iron stairs down to the parlor on the first floor. The scents of Korean cooking waft up to my apartment, a two hundred square foot studio with one tall narrow window that looks out over the alleyway. If I stand there I can watch a steady stream of men walk in and out of the parlor. Young and old, plump and thin, chubby boys and stooped graybeards, they all have one thing in common. Slumped shoulders and a faraway look. They know what they're about to do and when they come out they know what they've done. I drink whiskey from a chipped coffee mug and watch. I don't know how the mug came to be in my box of personal effects, the one they gave back when I was paroled. It was my father's, though. It's all that I have of him. For now.

I have a business meeting this afternoon in New York. I'll be catching a private jet in a few hours. I'm not sure if I'll be violating my parole or not. I'm allowed to travel for business.

First, I need to steal my car back.

This 'apartment' is about the size of my closet in the suite of rooms where I grew up.

Suits hanging on a rack, a cart like the use at a dry cleaner's, socks and underwear in a rubber tub, and a mattress covered in a plain white sheet. A refrigerator rattling away as it cools a block of Velveeta, a pack of imported ham, eight beers and a jar of peanut butter.

I don't even know why I keep the peanut butter in the fridge.

This is my life.

For now.

As I descend the rickety cast iron staircase I check my watch. It's a Timex I picked up at K-Mart after I stepped off the bus. I have to be on the flight in eight hours. It's now two thirty-three in the morning. The parlor closes at three, I think. That's when the in-and-out stream stops, or maybe the patrons are too scared to brave the mean streets at four in the morning. I don't know or care.

A stoop-shouldered man emerges and doesn't look at me and I don't look at him. I check my watch again and walk in the rain. It's a light drizzle that covers everything, makes the world glow. Water slides down my face and clings to my eyebrows. I glance at a shop window. The lights are shut off inside, and I see myself in a glass darkly. For a startling moment I'm walking side by side with my father's ghost, but I see the tattoos running down both arms to stop just above the wrist and it's just me. Dad never wore his hair this long and he never visited a tattoo parlor.

He had one tattoo, a crudely incised PETER in blue ink on his right shoulder. When he was a kid he and some boys he knew gave themselves tattoos with pins and a ballpoint pen. His was buried so deep in the flesh that all his attempts to remove it failed, and so he had his own name tattooed on his meaty shoulder until he died.

I should probably be wearing a jacket. November, and rain, but it's unseasonably warm, almost fifty. I've had enough of being confined. I want to swing my arms.

The car is parked in a lot. I stop to pay a bleary-eyed attendant and walk over. It's an unremarkable Toyota. I've been ordered to keep a low profile.

I hate driving this thing. The old city is dead at night. Last call was over an hour ago and the tourists get scared of the dark. It's one of the safer areas but all cities are the same. I fucking hate cities. Too much chain link and concrete and neon, not enough trees. I don't belong here.

Turn on 3rd onto Market, catch I-95. It's a straight run now. I obey all posted limits and traffic signals.

Have to. I'm on parole, after all. I wouldn't want to get pulled over on my way to steal a car.

Driving gives me a lot of time to think. My knuckles go white. The wheel creaks in protest.

I've had plenty of time to think.

That's what prison is. The punishment isn't confinement. They put a roof over your head. It's not isolation, either, unless you get sent to solitary. I never did. It's not following orders, it's not the shitty therapy groups, either. (Evidently, I have an anger management problem.) No, the punishment is *time*. Time to think, time to brood,

4

time to plan. When you're out in the world all you want is time. People say "there aren't enough hours in the day" and try to stretch them out.

In prison, the bars just keep you in. It's the time that punishes you.

Time has come today.

The drive takes almost an hour, out to Lancaster County, the very eastern edge. This is an old place. Everything around here is old. Old for the United States, anyway. I went to Europe once, went on a tour. Saw lots of history. Thousand year old buildings that just go about their business like buildings do. They're just *there*. Around here anything older than a century or two always goes behind velvet ropes. We think it's so special.

Europe. I was sixteen. There was good coffee and better company, but I can't think about that. If I try to hard I can't remember half the girls' names. I was never good at that to begin with. There was a time in my life when there were so many girls I'd have to take notes to remember who I fucked when. Then one day there were two girls. The one, and all the rest just kind of lumped together.

The windshield wipers tick away the seconds, minutes, an hour and a half or so. Take it easy in the rain.

From the mist, the high chimneys and glowing lights fold into existence, vague shapes growing more solid as I approach. It catches in my chest.

This is my home. I am going home.

Except I'm not. Now the high walls with their jagged glass tops and wrought iron spear points are there to keep me *out*, not *in*. My home no longer.

One of the oldest continuously occupied homes in the entire state, the Amsel estate is sprawling expanse of almost three hundred acres. *Kolonie,* my great-great-insert-more-greats grandfather named it. It's the German word for rookery. The family name, Amsel, means Blackbird. The house sits far back from the road, so far back, in fact, that in the deep gloom of a cloudy moonless night the only thing visible is the windows, like the distant lights of Xanadu or that green light in *The Great Gatsby.*

I didn't pay any attention in high school English, but I used to know somebody who cared a lot about that shit, and it meant I started caring about it, too.

If I keep driving half a mile there will be a break in the ancient brick wall that surrounds the wilds of the estate. The trees peel away and there's a huge wrought iron gate, almost fifteen feet tall, overtopping the wall itself by five feet. I've been casing the place for a while now. The new owners patched some broken places in the wall.

My ancestors coated the very top with broken glass, and the wall is also adorned with six inch long wrought iron spikes, each wickedly sharp. When they built the walls there was a real possibility the house might actually be attacked.

On top of the old school security system, there's all the modern conveniences. Motion sensors, cameras, and a pack of dobermans running on the property. Silent sentinels. I've always liked dobermans. They don't fuck around with barking, they just rip out your throat. If you toss them some sausage they'll eat it after they finish with you. Good, loyal, no nonsense dogs.

The place is a fortress, and with good reason.

It's old, though, and old houses have secrets. They start to love their families.

I could go on and on about my family. It used to be a huge extended network, all over the East coast. Distant relatives of mine fought on both sides of the Civil War, and both sides of the Revolutionary War, but only on one side of the French and Indian War. I can trace my ancestry back to a Hessian mercenary who switched sides and married into the family and took the Amsel name for himself, as the current patriarch at the time had only daughters. They did things like that back then.

Later on, the owners of the house were abolitionists, and the estate was a stop on the Underground Railroad. That's where I'm headed now.

I'm not sure who owns the farm that borders my family home, but the dilapidated barn is still there, edging up to the wall. I pull the Toyota off the road, bounce and jounce down a dirt track, and pull it right into the barn. I'm going to leave it here. It's not mine anyway, and after today I won't need it anymore. Four-thirty in the morning, now. Plenty of time, plenty of time. I leave the keys in the ignition and the doors unlocked.

Dad showed me this tunnel once. It still stands. In the barn, in the back corner, the half-rotted floorboard lifts up. The tunnel is dark, and barely tall enough for me to stand, bending my head a little. I take a flashlight and a stick. It's always full of spiders. I fucking hate spiders. Suffer not the arachnid to live. I think that's in the Bible somewhere.

If it's not, it should be.

The tunnel is sixty feet long, shored up with old timbers that are so hard they may as well be stone. It looks like a mine shaft in a cowboy movie. When I was a kid, I was terrified of this place. Of course, it's November and it's freezing cold at night, so the few times I have to knock down the web the one that made it is already dead, spindly legs curled up on themselves. I didn't need much encouragement to stay out of here when I was a kid but Dad made it very clear I wasn't ever to travel the tunnel alone; once he was younger then I was the first time he showed it to me, he found a nest of black widows and it was just luck that he didn't put his foot in it and get bitten half a hundred times. Probably would have killed him. Adults can usually survive the widow's bite, but not *that* many.

When I emerge from the other side I'm covered in dust and a little dirt and my stick is coated with filmy old spider silk.

I toss it aside and cut off the flashlight, then take a few minutes for my eyes to adjust.

I make it about twenty yards when the dogs show up.

They fold out of the darkness on silent legs, black specters with bobbed tails and cropped ears that make them look like silky black devils. I stop and they surround me, staring, silent. One by one they bare their fangs.

One of them is older than the others, gray hairs silvery on his dark face. He pads over, the stump of his tail twitching as he tries to wag. I crouch down and offer him my hand. He sniffs, and gives me a friendly lick as I scratch behind his ears.

"Hey, buddy," I whisper. "I wish I could remember which one you were."

The others take their cue from the leader, surrounded me and sniff at me and I pet them one by one. They'd rip out an intruder's throat and leave his rotting carcass to be found by the groundskeeper in the morning.

I'm not an intruder. The intruders are inside, sleeping in my *fucking* house.

One step at a time.

After I pay my respects to the dogs, I move silently through the grounds. This section is wooded, kept wooded to conceal the movements of runaway slaves and the new owners have let it run wild. There are oaks here that stood before the United States was the United States. Hell, the ivy growing on some of the trees is older than that. It's like walking through some ancient forest. Dobermans hadn't been developed yet but my grandfather's grandfather's grandfather probably walked these woods with a pack of hounds, just like I am now.

There used to be a path here but the stones are worn down smooth and covered with loam. I used to walk here all the time with my mother and father. When you're a kid, Mom and Dad are just *there*. Only now with both of them gone do I realize how I miss them both so fucking much. I can see them in my mind's eye on this very path on a warm autumn day, walking hand in hand. Dad was built like I am- tall and heavily muscled, but he kept his coal black hair closely cropped.

That was so long ago.

The garage is big enough to be a house on its own. A long, long time ago, it was a stables, but my grandfather, or maybe great grandfather, had it converted and rebuilt into a garage. His car, a lumbering Packard, is still in the furthest bay, or was when I was last here. I went for a ride in a few times. It's big and slow and ponderous to drive and I'm not here for it.

I'm here for my Dad's car. Technically, she's mine. They're holding her hostage here.

The garage is in sight, but so is the house. The lights are on on the second floor.

I shouldn't. I should go nowhere near it, not yet.

Refusing to listen to that little voice that says *you shouldn't* is probably how I ended up in prison for five years, but old habits die hard. I run across the grass, hoping I don't set off a motion detector or end up on camera. Stupid, stupid, stupid. I could end up back in prison serving out the rest of my term for this, plus interest, but I have to see.

I did this a dozen times when I was a kid. The back of the house is a huge terrace, with a roof supported by massive columns of real marble. They're so worn from age and acid rain that it's easy to shimmy right up. The pockmarks are like handholds, like the stippling and grippy spots on a climbing wall.

I was twelve when I did this the last time, but I'm in the best of shape of my life. Lots of weight lifting and constant body weight exercises in my cell, you see. It's easy to get up to the terrace roof, though I go on all fours where I used to run when I was a kid. Work my way across to the wall. A ledge runs all the way across the house, and these brick buttresses jut out from the sides. They're slick from the rain, so I take it easy, and work my way down the ledge, using the brick handholds. My old room is four windows down. The light is on inside. I stop by the window and lean over.

Evelyn walks out of the en-suite, wrapped in a towel. It's a creamy white towel, but it's darker than her skin, as pale as milk. When I first met her I thought she was an albino, but she's not. Real platinum blonde hair cascades to her hips in a perfectly straight fall. The water turns it green when she gets wet. I remember seeing that the first time, first time I ever saw her go swimming. She loves to swim.

She sits on the bed and takes a blow dryer to her hair, never once glancing at the window. She's more delicate than slender. I remember holding her wrists in my hands, feeling her long fingers lace through mine. I could stay here for hours and just watch. After running the hair dryer she starts brushing out her hair. I've never seen a shade quite like hers. It's what they call platinum blonde but it's almost silver, only a hint of gold in the right light. The only color is in her eyes, a striking blue. There's power in those eyes.

Eve is my stepsister. Her father married my mother when I was nineteen years old.

Then he sent me to prison and stole my life.

Now she sleeps in my bed.

I edge away from the window, carefully make my way across the roof and down the column. She's up early, but then, she was always an early riser. The light is still on, but the sun is coming up, bruising the eastern sky. I've been here too long, took too much of a risk.

I had to see her. It's been five years.

She stole my life, along with her rat bastard father. She eats my food, lives in my house, sleeps in my bed.

…Still.

I'm here for the car. That's my opening play. I sprint over to the garage. There's ten bays, the car is in bay four. It was always in bay four. My father treasured this automobile, did all the work on it himself and taught me everything he could; he died when I was twelve, so it wasn't much but I built on it as much as I could. I have more interest in being a mechanic than running a multinational business, but a man once wrote that what men want does not matter. Or women, I guess. The bay doors aren't locked. I roll up the door, and there she is.

They knew how to build 'em back then, Dad always said. She's a '70 Pontiac Firebird. She was born stock, but Dad did a load of work on her himself. All new running gear, topped off with a twin-turbo on a big block crate motor, four hundred cubic inches. State of the art disk brakes, all new steering, ivory pearl paint and a massive, multicolored screaming chicken decal on the hood. She's a beauty. Just touching the cool metal of the fender brings me back. I remember screaming my head off when Dad drove me in this car. Once I even overhead Mom joking with him when I wasn't supposed to be awake.

Yeah, that's right. I was *conceived* in the back seat of this car. It's as much my home as the house, if not more so, and it is mine.

Nobody bothered to lock the doors. Or drive her for a long time, from the dust in the interior. I flip open the glove compartment and pull out the registration.

Yup, VICTOR AMSEL. The address is wrong, but it's my fucking name. This is my car, legally, free and clear.

A quick trip over to the key box and I perform the only breaking of this breaking and entering operation, shearing off the rusted old padlock with some bolt cutter I find lying around. I take the key and the spare and slip back inside. The seat still fits me like a glove. They must have just dumped her here. Gas tank is empty, of course. Fortunately the garage has its own supply. I twiddle my thumbs until the tank is full, then finally get back in for the third time.

I turn the key. The motor chugs.

Oh, come *on*.

Another twist, and the *rrr—rrrr-rrrrrr* turns into a throaty note from the exhaust, but she doesn't turn over for me. Come on. One more time. Fuck that Toyota. No disrespect to the Japanese, but I want my car back. I want my house, my *life*.

Third time's the charm.

The roar of the exhaust sounds like an old airplane, thunderously loud in the confined space. The engine smoothes out almost immediately and I feel a surge of joy as I let out the clutch and ease in the gas. The car rumbles forward out of the garage and I whip around the turn, open the throttle and stab the button taped to the roof with my thumb. I hope the batteries aren't dead.

They're not, somehow. The wrought iron gates swing open. I roll the windows down. The rain has stopped and the air smells damp and musty. Mists cling to the ground.

I jam my hand out the window and give the security camera the finger before I whip out onto the road and two long black stripes of burnt rubber on the asphalt.

Vic is back, assholes.

Chapter Two

Evelyn

I wake up at four thirty in the morning, each and every day. My morning routine is absolutely the same, down to the minute. First I brush my teeth, then I floss, then I shower, dry and brush out my hair. My hair is, in my own opinion, my best feature. My skin is too pale and lined with blue and red veins. When I get out of the shower, I look like a roadmap from the scalding heat of the water and the freezing chill of a November morning in this ancient house.

My clothes for the day are already laid out. A dark blue pencil skirt, blazer and black blouse, dark stockings and sensible shoes. I wind my hair into a simple bun and lock it in place with a pair of chopsticks, black. As I said, my hair is my best feature, so I keep it plain, to match the rest of me. Otherwise I am far from remarkable, at least in a good way. My nose is too big, my face too narrow. I don't get much sleep and it shows on my face.

Breakfast is waiting for me downstairs. Father fired the Amsels' cook after Victor's mother passed away. He replaced most of the staff, in fact. I eat in the kitchen, skipping the overly ostentatious dining room. The cook, a round woman with a thick French accent, has little to say to me. Father keeps her around to impress clients. I eat a bowl of oatmeal and drink a glass of orange juice. The cook must love me. I eat the same thing for breakfast, lunch, and dinner, every day.

My assistant will be awake soon. After I've been served, the cook goes back to the servant's quarters, back to bed, leaving me alone in the kitchen. Every sound rings heavily off endless expanses of stainless steel. I hate this place; I feel like I'm coming here to be dissected every morning. I put my own dishes in the sink and walk upstairs to the office.

Peter Amsel -Victor's father- had a lovely Olde World office, in the very center of the house. I don't use that. My office was once a bedroom. The house has sixteen bedrooms, though I think the largest brood that ever lived here was a total of eight children. In the old old

old days, the Amsels used to house their entire brood here, generations living under the same roof. When Father married Victor's mother and I moved in here, they lived alone. The house felt cavernous, and it still does. It feels angry. I'm not a superstitious person. I don't believe in ghosts or any such foolishness. I don't care how old the house is, it's just brick and mortar, plaster and paint and wood.

It hates me anyway. I don't belong here.

One day I will approach father about disposing of the estate, but not yet.

I've broached the idea before. The problem is legitimacy. Through a series of rather unfortunate events, I have come to be the heir to the Amsel fortune. My own portfolio is modest, inheritance from my mother. The Amsel holdings make me a billionaire, the ninth richest woman on the planet.

Peter Amsel's will left everything to Victor, on certain conditions. When he went to prison, he was disinherited and it all reverted to his mother. His mother's will passed everything to me. When we lost her to cancer shortly after Victor's imprisonment, it all became mine. I'd give it all back if I could. I never wanted this.

I can still hear her breathy whisper. It was a terrible ordeal for her to speak with the cancer ravaging her lungs. Her last words were a throaty rasp.

Promise, was the last thing she said. Promise me.

I'm better at keeping my schedule than I am keeping promises.

Assistants are a pain. I go through them like a dog chewing bones. The latest is Alicia. She's the first one that hasn't complained about my hours. I let her sleep in- I don't expect her to meet me in the office until seven in the morning. She arrives without comment and sits down in the guest chair in front of my desk and spreads out my agenda on her lap. I prefer to keep everything on paper. Electronics are not secure. Alicia is a middle aged woman, a mother of three who needs my patronage. If I were a cruel person I would exploit that. I don't, I only ask for competence and that she refrain from wasting my time with pointless nonsense. I listen vaguely as she reads out my agenda for the day. I already know all of it. I need to be on a private jet in four hours, meaning we must leave in three. Before that I sit back and listen to her briefing for an hour as she goes over the news.

That damned feature story on me is causing no end of trouble. One of the financial rags interviewed me last month. They wanted me to show up in a cocktail dress and sprawl out on a desk, like a model in some kind of skin mag layout. I showed up in my usual conservative attire and stared into the camera. The magazine now sits on my desk, my own face staring back at me. I think they Photoshopped it, tried to make me prettier. I think I look like a weasel. Maybe a fox, if you're being charitable, but not in the vulgar sense. The screaming bold headline proclaims me the Ice Queen of Wall Street. I haven't read the article. I don't need to. If I was a man I'd be celebrated. I dare to do this and be a woman, so I must be lambasted for my arrogance.

As Alicia finishes the morning briefing I finger the edges of the paper. I have a distinct urge to ruin the career of everyone involved in printing this thing, from the editor all the way down to the copy boys in their mailroom. I could, if the urge struck me.

Amsel is a holding company. Long, long ago, the family got its start manufacturing explosives. Gunpowder, to be precise. The family estate borders a sloping quick running river that used to be lined with mills for miles, fueling the Union war machine while, ironically, some cousins fought on the confederate side. There was never a direct threat to these holdings, but there was a time when this house was strategically important. That ended a long time ago. Gunpowder became chemicals, chemicals became a dozen other products from solvents to adhesives to demolition explosives. Amsel helped in wars, put men on the Moon and create the Internet. Everyone talks about the innovations of this or that computer company but their devices would be useless without fifteen patents that belong to the family for the next sixty years, and in perpetuity if our lobbyists do their job. I can meet with Senators on a whim. Billionaires look busy when they see I'm coming.

None of this makes me feel anything.

I suppose that's my advantage.

Alicia has a file for me, my latest target.

They sell biscuits. Actually, powder that comes in boxes that mixes with milk and eggs to make biscuits. That's the flagship product. Thorpe Biscuit has expanded over the last twenty years into a food and food services empire. Ninety-five percent of the biscuits served in restaurants and eaten in homes are Thorpe and they have a good chunk of the food service industry and manufactured food markets under their control. Walk into a grocery store and something like ninety percent of the goods are produced by one of three companies, if you follow the ownership back up the chain. Thorpe is one of those, with the smallest market share of the big three. They do six billion dollars a year in revenue.

Yes, I yawn while I'm reading it.

They're screwed. The company is going under, due to total mismanagement. Thorpe is run by old money, Jim Thorpe III, great-grandson of the founder. I know more about him than he does. The dossier open on my desk reads like something an assassin would use to study a target. I know all of his habits, his movements. I know what he had for breakfast three weeks ago, what he gave his wife for Mother's Day and his mistress for Secretary's Day, which Ninja Turtle each of his children prefer (the youngest favors Donatello), the names of his boats. I even know about the funds he has squirreled away in Switzerland for when it all goes belly up under him.

I am not without mercy. I will allow him to remain on in some capacity at the company. He will continue to own stock. Today he will agree to a merger or I will launch my hostile takeover campaign. One word to Alicia and one of the six Amsel conglomerates will put in the maximum allowed bid on the open market for shares of Thorpe stock, as permitted by the Williams Act. At the same time, I will contact the large shareholders I've been meeting with for what's known as a *proxy fight*. They will vote for me. I don't even need them all. I already indirectly own twenty percent of the common stock through a pension fund group under Amsel control. Jim Thorpe is, to put it colloquially, screwed. I scratch at the papers with my close-cut fingernails. It feels like sharpening my claws.

Once the company is mine the challenge of fixing it might at least make me feel something.

Six years. That's the last time I felt something, I think.

The morning's work is boring, mostly answering emails, correcting other people's mistakes, gathering intelligence, arranging for the sell off of an underperforming holding and sending orders to my other assistants to bring me information on new acquisitions. The lawyer will be joining me in New York to meet with Thorpe.

Once everything is arranged, it's time to go.

When I step out of the office, the head of security is waiting for me.

His name is Harrison Carlisle and he's one of the biggest men I've ever seen. Almost seven feet tall and three hundred pounds of muscle. He comes from some little town up the Susquehanna river. I think his cousin or his uncle or some such thing is a police officer up there. Harrison was a Marine and then a private military contractor. I remember the name of the town, now. Paradise Falls. One of my college roommates was from up there. Jennifer, her name was. There must be something in the water in that town; she towered over me. When I lived with her I always felt like I was in her shadow. She was stunning, with a gymnast's slender build, a models' grace, and she was absolutely gorgeous, but she was dating some local boy that went to the same school as us and never talked to anyone else. She rarely talked to me, for that matter. I haven't thought about her in a long time.

Something in the air this morning brings nostalgia.

"Ma'am," Harrison grunts, knocking me out of my reverie.

Good. I don't want to think about college. I don't want to think about Victor. Not that it ever stops me. Every day for five years, I-

"One of the cars was stolen this morning."

I blink a few times. I glance at Alicia. I look at Harrison again.

"What?"

"Somebody broke into the garage and took it."

"Yes," I sigh, "That's what *stolen* means. Which one?"

"The Pontiac."

An ice cube slides down my back and I go rigid. There's one Pontiac in the Amsel collection. A packard, a Rolls Royce, a 1958 Plymouth Fury, half a dozen less valuable cars and Victor's mother's Hyundai, and one Pontiac, that ludicrous beast Victor's father passed down to him.

"I assume you've contacted the police."

Harrison nods.

"Deal with it. Call my father, get more men, double the details. I want foot patrols again. Those damned dogs aren't doing their job."

"Yes, ma'am."

My security chief leaves and I let out a slow breath. I should tell him. Victor loved that car, he'd be crushed to hear it's been stolen. I can't imagine why someone would break into the grounds and steal that car. It's one of the least valuable in the collection. Victor once explained it to me; the numbers don't match, whatever that means, because of his father's modifications. The Rolls Royce, a Phantom II, is worth a small fortune on its own. Why would someone steal the Firebird and leave the others undisturbed?

I suppose I should feel violated. I've been robbed. My home has been defiled.

Except it's not my car and it's not my house, and it's not my car, it belongs to Victor. I don't care about his damned car. If I never saw it again I would not mind in the least.

Promise!

"Ma'am?"

Alicia stares at me. I realize I've been standing around for a good minute staring into space. I shake my head.

"We're on a timetable. Have the car brought up."

I don't drive very often. Father pays drivers for that. The BMW sedan out front is my birthday present from last year, not that I care all that much. As long as they run, one car is the same as another to me.

I slip into the back seat and stare out the window as Alicia works, answering emails and contacts that are not sufficiently important for my extremely valuable time. I spend a good hour of that time brooding in the car, saying nothing, trying to think of anything but Victor.

My louse of a stepbrother. Even thinking about him makes me furious. I loathe him, after what he did to me.

That was another life, that happened to another person. She's dead.

Long live the ice queen.

The ride to the airport is about an hour. I'm not flying by airline, 'with the rabble' as my father would say. We have a private jet, a sleek black Gulfstream. My seat inside is enormous and plush, and once my seatbelt is on and the plane is in the air, I feel comfortable catching an hour or so of sleep. It's a short hop from Philadelphia International to LaGuardia, and it feels like no time has passed at all when Alicia wakes me with a gentle, but insistent, "Ma'am."

I don't suffer anyone to touch me. One of my assistants once presumed to shake me by the shoulder in a situation like this. I don't know what she does for a living now. I don't much care.

I snap awake, glad I didn't dream. After landing I take a minute to sip a cup of black coffee and exit the plane, to a waiting town car. Alicia knows better than to chatter. The driver does not. I silence him with a curt look and watch mostly identical buildings glide by my window. New York traffic is annoying but I am never late. *Late* implies there will be some consequence for my failure to arrive on time. They will wait for me. My lips curl in a hint of a smile.

I keep trying to feel something. It's not working.

After perhaps forty-five minutes for a few miles of driving, the town car pulls into the garage. Thorpe has sent some chattery underling to meet me. He extends a hand, I walk past him, Alicia in tow. One of the lawyers follows. Sline, I think his name is. Something like that. The others shy away from me in the elevator, even the underling charged with turning the key to take me to the private upper floors for the meeting. I don't look at any of them. The ride up is quick, the doors open, and I walk through the executive offices. The doors are open, the occupants all look up as I pass, shivering as I walk by. The boardroom is at the far end. I suppose I should be impressed. The view is magnificent, a panoramic, one hundred eighty degree expanse of city skyline and Hudson river. I'm not impressed. I've seen it.

Thorpe is waiting for me.

I size him up. I've seen pictures. This is the first time we've met in person.

Jim Thorpe is about five eight, soft and round but not fat, and looks like old money. They all look the same.

Except Victor. Victor looks like a model.

Be quiet, little voice.

He offers me a soft hand. I deign to shake it, and resist the urge to wipe my hand on my jacket. Alicia discretely hands me an antibacterial wipe as she spreads out our materials at the head of the long conference table.

I'm good at reading people. Thorpe is scared. He knows why I'm here, he knows he needs me, and he wants to sleep with me. I try to ignore the last part. It's not me, it's a power thing. Two-thirds of the executives I meet are obviously picturing me naked. It's a defense mechanism. They can't be afraid of a woman, so that's what they make themselves see. It's hard to feel predatory and afraid at the same time.

"Pleasure to make your acquaintance, Ms. Ross," he says in a voice that holds no hint of pleasure. "Glad you could be here."

"Quite. The others?"

"The board will be arriving shortly, I'm sure."

"Good. That will give me a few minutes to set up. Alicia."

There's a podium at the head of the table. I can tell Thorpe is used to sitting there from the look he gives me when I claim his seat. My face is as still as tranquil waters, but inside I feel a hint of satisfaction. A secretary appears and hands him some files. I recognize her from the pictures the private detective sent me. She's the one he beds when his favorite is out of town. What do you call it when a man has something on the side and is cheating on his mistress? A double mistress? There should be a word for that, if there isn't already. Thorpe stands there awkwardly, eyeing me as I lay out my papers. Alicia has our projector in a case and sets it up, wires it to the laptop and aims it at the wall. I sip from a bottle of water and roll my shoulders.

Here they come. The board of directors. I've already spoken with half of them and I control enough of an interest in the company to be one. I'm about to make the case that their current chairman is an idiot and is running the company into the ground and I can save it.

Six of them file in.

Then a seventh.

Victor Amsel.

The room is utterly silent.

Chapter Three

Victor

I walk into the room and lock eyes on Evelyn.
She's frozen, still as a statue, staring at me. Her
eyes trace me to my seat as I sit down at the end
of the table and rest my attache on the wood. I
run my hands over the tabletop. Antique, I think.
I'll bet it's as old as the company. The top is
perfectly smooth, polished to a high mirror shine.
Evelyn's reflection is dark and wavy in the
surface. Her mousy little assistant doesn't seem
to know the score, from the way she looks at her
boss. Evelyn recovers, her face going still. I've
seen that mask before. Her face just sorts of goes
blank. Models do that when they run the
catwalk, just go still. Your gaze could slide right
off her face, except for her eyes. They're razor
sharp, and somehow in the middle of that
neutral expression is a cutting look.

"Why is he here?" she says, calmly, clearly
meaning me.

"He was invited," says Thorpe.

He toys with his suit coat as he sits down, and looks around with a smile.

"Gentlemen, I'm not going to lie," he says, smiling at his board, his friends. They'd all cut his throat, but everybody in business is always friends. "We're in trouble, here."

Business is the art of pissing on people with a smile, my Dad used to tell me.

Trust me, I'd rather be elbow deep in an engine block right now, but alas. I drum my fingers on the briefcase.

"Miss Ross," he says, turning to Evelyn. "Care to begin?"

"After he leaves." She's never taken her eyes off of me. Her face is a mask but her tones are acid.

"He's been invited here by the board," Thorpe says. He shifts uncomfortably under Evelyn's icy gaze.

She looks at me again, and her perfect mask cracks into a scowl.

"This man is a convicted felon. You may have missed it, Mr. Thorpe, but he went to prison for embezzlement and insider trading."

"It was only medium security."

Evelyn has the most pretty lips. She doesn't wear makeup. They're a pale soft pink, and she's cute when she sneers, no matter what anybody says. It makes me smile. I can't help it.

I hate you, you bitch, I think to myself, *stop being cute.*

The innocent girl I knew was a lie. She was always her father's creature. A thief in the night who stole my life. They took my home, my legacy, even my mother. They ruined me. I have to remember that. I have to.

Silence has stretched from brief to uncomfortable.

Thorpe clears his throat. "He's staying. Were you going to begin, Ms Ross, or do we need to hear what he has to say first?"

Her face flushes up to her hairline.

Damn it, Eve. Stop being so pretty.

"Very well. Alicia."

God this shit is boring. Evelyn spends the next hour reiterating reports and data and sales figures, all publicly reported and freely available, she stresses repeatedly. Every time she mentions contacting Thorpe she throws in a line about talking to his secretary. The change in her tone, the flutter of skin around her eyes is very subtle, but it's there. She knows, and Thorpe knows she knows. The tension in the air is like the presence of hornets. You heard the fuckers buzzing and then they stopped, and you just know they're there. The presentation is mostly for Thorpe's benefit, the real message between the lines, and that message is: You are my bitch, bitch. She's getting off on this, or she's trying to, anyway. She keeps a bunch of papers on the little podium, and spends half as much time giving me a death glare as she does actually addressing the board.

The point of all of it is this: Thorpe is going into a death spiral. Their suppliers are raising prices, their distributors are raising prices, the union is threatening a strike, and there's a new regulatory issue the company hasn't yet dealt with. Something about the way the boxes are labeled, a new rule about calories and nutrition facts or something. None of the details matter. The point is, the money coming in is already not enough to cover costs; the costs are bloated. Evelyn stops just shy of helping them, smirks at her own expertise. When she does she looks wicked and wanton.

I keep forgetting I'm supposed to hate her.

Yet I don't understand her. The Evelyn I remember was wide-eyed and shy, terrified of the world around her, sheltered. The Eve I remember needed me. This... this *ice queen* doesn't. The presentation reminds me of a cat playing with its prey, without even planning to eat it. This is all a game to her.

She looks a lot like her father.

My hands squeeze into fists.

"Amsel has considerable resources to bring to bear to correct these deficiencies," she says, beginning her close. "I am not planning to swoop in and replace everyone. Yes, some bloat will need to be shed. Many of your business practices will change, but what I am proposing today is a partnership, not a takeover."

The takeover would come if they defy her, I realize. It's in her tone, the subtle way she moves. Everyone in this room is a guppy, in a tank with a shark. I can see it on three of the six board member's faces. They're already convinced. She probably took care of this well before this meeting started. If I were a more hateful man my first thought would be she slept with one or all of them, but Eve would never do that. Or maybe I just want to believe that. She was so shy, so fragile. I wonder where that girl went and where this creature came from, with her skin as hard as ice and her sharp claws.

In the same neutral voice she begins laying out the terms, and what Amsel has to offer. It's very generous, if you're an idiot. She's asking them to put themselves in her hand, and the only person who cares less about any of these men than each other is Evelyn. If they're smart they've studied and if they studied they know she's going to give the company six months to turn around or gut it and pour the money from selling off the equipment into another takeover like this.

One company in five that Amsel has acquired since Eve took over the company has been broken down and sold off to competitors. I wonder if she ever thinks about the consequences of her actions. My father would be disgusted at what his name has come to represent in the circles he traveled. A shell of a company run by a frigid bitch on one side, his ex-con son on the other, a walking embarrassment to the family. God knows I did enough embarrassing shit in my youth, but who doesn't?

"Thank you, Ms. Ross. We'll take it under consideration," Thorpe says.

There's a note in his voice she doesn't like, by her scowl.

"You may remain if you like, to hear the counter offer."

I'm not going to lie. That was definitely my idea.

I saunter up to the podium and open up my attache. I don't have a projector, nor do I have a presentation. Instead I pass out folders. Thorpe has already seen the proposal, this is for the rest of the board. They open and I see their reaction when they lay eyes on what I'm proposing.

"Eve has done a good job of explaining why you're screwed, so I'll spare you a retread of the gory details." I shoot her a glance. "Thanks, by the way. You saved me from talking myself raw."

"Young man," one of the older board members says, "I don't appreciate your tone."

"I'm not here to sell you my tone. I'm here to save you from her."

They all look at Eve. She shrinks just a little into her chair, her eyes wide. When Eve gets mad, her eyes go wide and she tucks her bottom lip under her teeth. She does that now, and her hands go white as she grips the arms of her chair. Whiter, anyway. She's furious.

Good.

"The details are in the papers I've provided. Bottom line is this. I want thirty percent of the common stock, for which I am prepared to pay generously."

"With what?" Evelyn snaps. "What do they pay you in prison, a dollar a day to stamp license plates?"

"Miss Ross," Thorpe says, a hint of warning in his voice.

All the color, such as it is, drains from Evelyn's face. It's been a long time since anyone but her father has taken that kind of tone with her. I can read it plain as day in her face.

"I've provided all the necessary information for your due diligence. My plan is a more hands off approach than Eve's. I'm not here to eat your company alive, I'm here to keep it afloat. The union and your creditors will get what they want. In addition to market price for the stock, the group I represent will extend an interest-free line of credit to cover Thorpe's liabilities for the next two years."

"This is absurdly generous," another of them says. "What's in it for you?"

"It'll pay off when I triple the price of your stock, and I will."

"How?"

"I'd rather not say in front of the competition, but look at the terms. If the stock price does not in fact triple by the one year anniversary of the day you sign the papers, all the stock I purchase reverts back to you. I'm going to bet with my money that we can turn this around."

"Who's we?" the old man says. "Ross has a point. Did you dig out of your prison cell with a spoon and find a treasure chest?"

I smile at him where Eve would wither him with a look.

"No, but my father's name used to mean something in the financial world and I want it to mean something again. I called a lot of friends, all of whom have been burned by what used to be my father's company. Again, all the information you need to make an informed decision is in the packet I passed out. Look, I know I'm asking you to do homework on a Friday…"

Four of them chuckle softly.

Gotcha.

"…but it's me or her. Do I need to tell you what happens if you hand over the reins to her? My plan involves bringing in consultants. Her plan involves removing your entire management staff and replacing them with her cronies. She'll increase your efficiency, alright. She'll fire the union workers, close down the plant and hire scabs somewhere else. She'll cancel contracts with your suppliers and start using substandard product from suppliers she controls. She'll stick knives in your backs from a dozen directions and squeeze out as much profit from the company as she can until the reputation of the brand is ruined, and when it's not making money anymore she'll exercise her rights to tear it all apart and sell everything off to pay off the company's creditors, which if you research the matter, you will find all belong to her. She's already got you in her jaws. When you sign her papers she'll shake you and snap your neck. My plan is a way out. If we fail, you'll be no worse off than if you sign on with her and go under the Amsel umbrella. If you say no she'll start the wheels on a hostile takeover. She probably already has."

Evelyn is staring daggers into me.

"This is a lot to consider," Thorpe says.

Evelyn looks at him, then at me. She rises abruptly from her seat and leaves her assistant to frantically gather their materials. I look around the room.

"Questions?"

"We'll reach a decision soon, I think," says Thorpe.

"I'll be waiting."

I give them a winning smile, grab my attache and stride out.

Evelyn is in the hallway.

"You son of a bitch," she hisses. "How dare you-"

Before I can think, before I can plan, my hand lashes out and I seize the collar of her blouse. Her feet barely touch the floor as I drag her out of the hall into another conference room. She rakes her nails over the back of my first and I let go. She looks at me, looks at the door, and goes for it. She doesn't make it halfway before I drag her back by the arm and yank the door shut and twist the lock. She rounds on me with a savage backhand that actually flashes my lights. I taste blood in my mouth from a split lip.

"Fucking let go of me," she snaps. "I'll scream."

"You promise?"

"Let *go!*"

"Eve, listen to me."

"I don't want to hear your lies. Get your hands off me, Victor. I loved your mother. That's the only reason I'm not going to have you back in prison *today*. Only if you let go of my arm."

I give her a little shake. Her eyes burn into me, and as my throat clenches with fury I feel my cock stiffen. God, she's beautiful.

"Let. Go," she repeats.

"No."

"Get off of-"

Before she finishes the sentence I have her up against the wall, my lips crushed against hers. It's been so goddamn long, almost five years since I've touched a woman. Hell, for five years I didn't even *smell* a woman. If you told me maybe ten years ago I'd go five years without a good lay I'd tell you I'd be fucking everything that moves when I was done.

All I want is her.

There's not even a moment of resistance. She kisses me back hard, hungrily, so hot. It's like swallowing a warm spoonful of honey. Whoever called her the ice queen was dead wrong. Her skin burns under my hands. I slip my arms under her jacket, feel her heat under her silk blouse. The feeling reminds me of slipping under a blanket with her, feeling her warmth against me as we lay intertwined.

One hand moves up her stomach and I squeeze her breast through blouse and bra, and she moans softly in to my mouth. Her hands stop pulling at my blazer and instead start hiking up her skirt, up over her hips. Jesus, there's already a wet spot on her underwear. She starts pushing them down, I pull them down, rip them to her knees and slide my hand between her legs. Her arousal is slick on my fingers, but I just hold her, cup my hand against her sex. A soft sound escapes her lips and she bucks and rolls her hips, grinding on my hand. I push her into the wall and slip my arm around her as her arms wrap around my neck.

My cock is raging, iron hard. I want to fuck her so bad. I could fuck her right here on the floor, I don't care. I want to explode inside her, feel her quiver around me as I make her cum. My finger slides inside her and it comes back to me, like muscle memory. I know *exactly* where and how to touch her to get the reaction I want, sliding my finger against just the right spot while I move my palm against her clit. She hugs me tighter and pushes her chin in to my shoulder, trembling. Her leg lifts up. All I have to do is get these pants down and get inside her. I have *never* been this hard.

I want to fuck her but I want to taste her more. I drop to my knees and she knots her fingers in my hair, pushes me forward as her hips cant towards me, and I suck on her clit as I slip a second finger into her body and start pumping, finger fucking her while I eat her pussy. She never makes a sound, no louder than a squeak or a sharp inhalation, but she's so fucking wet I think I might need to roll up my sleeve, a silly thought in the absurd joy of her taste. She tastes and smells just like I remember and I pull my hand away to clamp down on her hips with both hands and bury my face in her hot, sopping wet cunt. I want to get my tongue inside her. She's shaking now, barely in control of herself, and claps one hand over her mouth. Her other is twisting my hair so hard it hurts.

Just like old times. She used to pull my hair, scratch my back until I bed and beg me *more, more*. A few times she even bit me.

"Please," she pleads in a breathy voice, before pressing her hand to her mouth.

Her eyes are wide open.

I ease off. No, not yet. She's not allowed to cum until I want her to. My fingers enter her again as I stand up, yank her hand away and she kisses me as I pin her to the wall and very, very slowly slide my fingers forward and back, curling them just a little to make her knees shake. I swallow her moans as my tongue invades her mouth. I make her taste her pussy while I pleasure her. Her legs are shaking like leaves now, her stomach trembles, and her nails dig into my arms.

Cum. Cum for me you fucking bitch.

Her pussy squeezes my fingers. I just hold them there, feeling the heat and pulses and wetness. She never makes a peep, but her body goes rigid, softens a little, goes rigid again in spasms as her eyes unfocus, look past me. I hold her against me.

It's not fucking fair. Just let me love you, God damn it. Why can't I? Why did this have to happen?

"Vic," she purrs, trying to side her arms around me. "Victor..."

"I didn't do it," I bark at her, my voice strained. Christ, I'm a grown man on the verge of tears. "Eve, please believe me..."

She gives me a hard shove and I step away from her as she struggles to keep her feet, skirt hike dup over her ass, her sodden underwear quivering between her bowed knees.

"You son of a bitch, why did you bring it up?"

"Eve-"

"Beg my forgiveness," she snaps, standing to her full height, such as it is. "Beg me to forgive you, Victor."

My hand falls to my side.

"You're the one that should be begging my forgiveness," I snarl. "I never *touched* that girl. I never did any of it. All I ever wanted…"

"Liar," she says, coldly. "You're a filthy fucking liar, and I hate you. Don't ever touch me again."

She stumbles away, and suddenly I feel embarrassed to see her like this as she yanks her underwear up and pulls her skirt down.

"I hate you," she says, as I open the door.

Chapter Four

Evelyn

"I hate you," I snarl as he steps out.

The door slams behind him and I choke out the words in a tiny voice.

"Don't leave me."

Victor, come back. Victor *please*, I'm sorry, I'll forgive you, just come back.

Ten minutes later Alicia finds me sitting on the floor in a strange conference room, hugging my legs to my chest and sobbing.

"Ma'am…"

"Go away," I choke out. "Leave me alone."

"I can't. We need to leave. They're talking about calling security to remove you."

I stare at her. She's all blurry and I don't know why. Maybe it has to do with the hot burning on my cheeks. Water, there's water. Oh God, I'm crying. If Father saw me he'd… he'd…

I surge to my feet and stumble. My body is still shaking through the aftershocks. I haven't cum so hard since… since the last time Victor fucked me. I want him inside me.

Please come back.

I meant it, dam him. If he just told me the truth and asked me to forgive him, I would. I'd forgive him for the money, for Brittany, for all of it. I don't want any of this. I want him.

Yet I still hate him. I gave him everything and he crushed it in his hand and threw it away for the next piece of ass.

You stupid, immature, idiotic little girl. How dare you let yourself crack like this. Get up.

Alicia offers me a tissue. I snatch it and wipe down my face. I take a minute to smooth my hair and stride out of the conference room. There's building security approaching, rent-a-cops in cheap uniforms, but one look and they get out of my way as I almost dive into the elevator, tempted to tell Alicia to take the fucking stairs and just get *away* from me. All I can see is their eyes on me. Victor is right, damn him. They all hate me. Alicia despises me, the staff hates me. No one in the whole world wants me. I just want to curl up in a ball and disappear.

We were so happy once.

Head down, suppressing sobs, I rush back to the car, yank the door open and throw myself inside. Alicia follows, closes the door. No one says a word on the way back to the airport. When we arrive I trudge up the stairs and back to my seat, sink into it and close my eyes, but sleep won't come. I grip the armrests tightly during the ascent, calming only when the plane levels out. Sleep, dreamless or not, flees from me. My body still pulses with need. Victor, Victor, Victor. The way he held me while he… it was like he used to. He would hold me so tight, shelter me in those big arms of his. In the dark the tattooed feathers running up and down his arms would seem to shimmer, like some kind of dark secret gold. They ran from just above his wrist to his shoulders, spread over his back on the shape of wings. On his chest the screaming visage of a black bird stared out. I remember touching every line, every stitch of shading.

I hate myself.

The flight feels nine hours long, even though the ascent and descent are longer than the flight time, almost. A short hop. It's dark when the plane turns and tips back to descend into Philadelphia. As dark as it gets. Lights flood the world below, a galaxy on the ground drowning out the one in the sky. None of it means anything to me. I watch the ground swell up to meet us and some part of me wishes it would just crush the plane and end this misery. A taste, a touch, is worse than nothing at all. Victor's infuriating presence, the hate in his voice. If he only hated me I could survive it, but the touched me so tenderly, kissed me so fiercely. It was like he forgot he hated me. I forgot how much I hate him. I have to remember. Her name is Brittany. She was the next notch on his bedpost, and that's all I ever was. It was all lies, the whispered declarations, the promises. He turned around and mouthed the same words to someone else.

By the time I walk to the car I feel the venom of my hatred coming back, swelling cold and acid in my chest. He'll trick me. He tricked me before. I will never let anyone do that to me again. No one will ever get under my skin again. My skin is ice, harder than steel, and beneath it is only more ice. The cold settles in me during the ride and I feel almost composed when we returned to the house. I glance over and see the police outside the garage and it hits me, and the ice cracks.

It was him. Damn it, it was him, he was *here*. He took the car. Fine, let him. I hate the damned thing. Sitting there reminding me of what used to be. He can go to hell and take the car with him.

Weariness has settled into my bones by the time I emerge from the car. I stink of acidic sweat and other things and I feel like I've been stretched out, like taffy. I need a shower and I need a full night's sleep. I glance at Alicia, who has been silent since we left the offices.

"I'm taking tomorrow off."

She nods curtly, makes a note and veers away from me as I head upstairs, leaning on the bannister. I yawn as I reach the top of the stairs, scrub my hands through my hair and half stumble through the door into my room.

There I freeze.

My father is waiting for me. He stands in the room like a statue, frozen still. Like me he's pale all over but for blue eyes, like he's been carved from stone. He wears dark slacks and a white shirt. His tie is loosened. A withering look sends me a step back, but I swallow and step into the room, force myself to stand straight up.

"Did you fuck Victor Amsel?"

57

"No."

"Don't lie to me, Evelyn."

"I didn't have sex with him." I leave off the *today*. It's implied.

It's a technicality. There's a subtle twitch around his left eye. He knows.

"The show you put on today was quite a spectacle, apparently. It was on all the news sites. They were talking about you on television."

I swallow.

"I'm told it was tweeted," he says, with a sneering disdain.

I swallow again. "I'm sorry…"

"He played you like a tin fiddle. What do you have to say for yourself?"

"I don't… I didn't…"

The slap comes so fast I can't see it coming. One moment I'm standing. The next, pain explodes through my jaw, the world goes white in a flash, and I'm on my knees, leaning on one hand and clutching my face with the other. He gave me a savage backhand, knocked me right off my feet. When the daze ends I scrabble back against the wall, slide along to a corner and curl up, trembling. It's been a long time since he's hit me. Not since I was a girl.

"If he shows his face in your presence again, you will alert me immediately. In the meantime, I will begin working to ensure he's sent back to prison."

I nod.

"Yes, sir."

"You have work to do tomorrow. I will expect you to be discreet about your face."

He means the bruise rising on my skin. That's all he has to say. He gives me a look that makes me wilt, and walks out the door, pulling it shut behind him. As soon as it closes I scramble to my feet, seize a chair from the vanity table by the bathroom door and haul it over. I shove the antique wood under the doorknob and rush into the bathroom. I climb in the shower and turn it on, crying out as the cold water hits me, but silent as it turns scalding hot and steam swirls around me as I sink down to sit on the floor of the tub and curl up in the fetal position. My face is throbbing. Even my teeth hurt. It's been years and years since he knocked out one of my teeth, and it was only a baby tooth. He stopped hitting me when I turned ten, and switched to the belt. That stopped two years before he remarried, except for the one time.

Maybe ten minutes, maybe an hour later I half-crawl out of the tub and sit on the floor for a while. I'm mostly clean; a scalding hot shower will do that. I've turned pink from the heat and my fingers are all crinkly. I stand in front of the mirror and stare at myself. All I can see is the ugly purple bruise on my cheek. It's a bad one. It hurts, a lot. I should put something cold on it, but I don't care. After I stumble out of the bathroom and wrap myself up in a towel, I fall on the bed and stare up at the ceiling. The ceilings are surprisingly low in here, the windows huge. Outside it's started raining again and the water spritz the window and makes tiny tapping noises. The only other sound is my breathing. The staff are either in bed or gone home by now. I should eat, but the very idea of food makes me sick. I lay on my side, and think. I will have to cancel any appointments that require a face to face meeting tomorrow. Phone and email only. Everyone here knows not to ask how my face was marked.

I hate you, Victor. You said you'd save me from this.

A glance to the side, and I start staring at the bookcase. I don't know why I do this to myself. Wrapping up in a robe, I pad over to it on bare feet, reach for the top shelf and pull down the photo album. It's a cheap one, just vinyl over cardboard and binding rings. I sit back on the bed and spread it open on my lap.

The oldest pictures have my mother in them. I have my father's coloring but my mother's eyes, and the resemblance between us is uncanny even though she had dark hair.

I never knew her. She died in a car accident when I was three. Sometimes I can feel her, but not remember her. The pictures depress me, so I gingerly turn the plastic page. There are no photos of my father, either with me or alone. In fact there are no photos of me at all until I'm already in college. No birthdays or soccer practice or recitals or school plays. I was homeschooled until I went to college, and tutored; I played no sports. Father paid a personal trainer for me starting when I was thirteen. He would be disappointed in me now, I think. I don't eat much but I don't exercise anymore. There's no time. I'm falling behind on work even now. There are tasks on my schedule, but I can't stop staring at the pictures. Victor took most of them, and of course I am the subject. The backdrops are the main difference. There I am at the mall, there I am at the beach, there I am at the park. There are some selfies, from before they called them selfies. Victor points the camera at us.

A sob chokes out of my throat.

There's a few other pictures. Victor took a picture of me with my first roommate. Brennan, that was her name. Jennifer Brennan. I run my finger over the plastic covering the photo and wonder whatever happened to her. We were cordial, never friends. Jennifer was a strange one, even more shy and awkward than I was and she had a terrible phobia of anyone seeing her naked that made living in a small rectangular room with her rather difficult at times.

There's a picture of her boyfriend in here, too. What as his name? Francis, I think. It started with an F. Nice guy. I never kept in touch with Jennifer. If I called her tonight, would she have any idea who I am? Probably not. Nor would my second year roommate. I remember her; Christine Moore. I can't remember his name, but her boyfriend was pre-med and they were inseparable. I tap the picture of Christine a few times. I know what happened to her, I remember seeing it on the news, now. She went missing in Las Vegas a few years ago. I remember her mother weeping on the news.

Christine was a sweet girl. A little weird, but very kind. She didn't deserve whatever happened to her.

Another turn of the page. I roomed alone in my last year, at least officially.

Unofficially, Vic was living with me.

If my father found this album, he'd burn it. Thankfully he doesn't bother to go through my things.

One of the last pictures shows me sleeping. I'm lying on my side, and if my bare shoulder isn't hint enough, I know I'm naked under the blankets. There's a small, secret smile on my face. A hand reaches from behind the camera. It's Victor's soft touch on my cheek that makes me smile in my sleep. I remember that night.

How did it come to this?

I slam the book closed, surge over to the shelf and shove it back in its space. Quickly, I dress in pajamas and storm out of the room. The house is dark, empty. I don't know where I'm going except that I can't stay in that room anymore. I pace up and down the hall, and the portraits on the walls stare at me. The Amsels are an old family. It was their custom to have a portrait painted of the family patriarch in the prime of his life. The last one is Victor's father. I can't meet his eyes, even if they're only canvas. As I pace back the eyes weigh on my neck, cracked painted gazes burning me with recrimination. This is not my place. I do not belong here.

I don't belong anywhere.

The office. The door swings open. Not my office, the old one. It's huge, and has the highest ceiling of any room on the second floor, almost twelve feet. It actually pokes up into the attic. A ladder from the floor leads up to a walk around, just wide enough for one person. The entire top half of the room is bookcases, except for a door that heads up to the huge cupola that sits in the center of the roof. There's a widow's walk up there, too. Victor showed me once when he still lived here, and during the summers we would use it as a place to sneak away for a while and hide. The office itself is beautiful, with a real person carpet and a massive battleship of a mahogany desk, so long and wide it would make a fine bed if someone wanted to sleep on it.

For the most part, the room is untouched. After Victor's father died, his mother essentially kept it as a shrine to him, right down to the stack of papers he was working on the day he was killed. Victor treated this like a holy place. He used to come in here and brood, never touch anything, just sit in his father's chair and stare at the desk as if it held some kind of an answer for him. I never asked him what he was thinking about.

I think I know.

The shelves feel like they're going to topple in, dump their contents on my head and crush me. I rush back out into the hall, down to the stairs and though to the foyer. I could run outside but I hate those fucking dogs.

I end up in the kitchen, fixing myself a sandwich. Then Alicia walks in.

I blink a few times.

"What are you doing here?"

She flinches, and immediately turns to leave.

"Wait. I didn't mean it like that."

"Oh. Your father caught me as I was leaving and told me to make sure...." She trails off. "Oh my God. What happened?"

It's like an electric shock.

"Nothing. I fell down. Slipped in the shower. Tired."

She eyes me with a neutral expression.

"If you say so."

"What time is it?"

"Nine thirty."

"You should be home by now. Your kids."

She looks genuinely confused. I can see the response even if she's terrified to say it. *What do you care?*

"Have you eaten?"

Alicia eyes me. "No, I haven't."

"Want something?"

She looks at me like I just sprouted a second head.

"I..." she looks around, and actually hugs herself.

"I could stay for a minute," she says, quickly.

She moves to the fridge, but I shoo her away. I put the sandwich I was fixing myself in front of her and make my own, sit down at the table and take a small bite. I don't make very good sandwiches. I probably should have put some mayonnaise on the bread or something, but I can't find it.

"Are you alright?"

Her question startles me. Her reaction is instantaneous. Her mouth clicks shut and she looks down.

"No. I'm not."

"You were upset this afternoon."

"Yes."

"Not about the meeting."

"No. Not about the meeting."

She takes a bite, chews it slowly and swallows without looking up.

"Old flame," she says. It's not a question.

"Yes."

"Okay."

I look at her.

"I'm not going to say anything else. I heard you fired an assistant for touching your shoulder when you fell asleep on the plane."

"Yes. I did. They all hate me, don't they?"

Her sandwich is shaking. Her hands are, too.

"You can answer me. I asked you the question, so I must want the answer."

"Yes."

"Do you?"

"Sometimes. Please. I have three kids."

"I know. You're not fired. I'd offer to wrap that up so you can take it home but I don't know where the cook keep things to wrap up food."

"Thanks. I'm not really hungry. Can I go?"

"Yes. Come in at nine tomorrow. I'm sleeping in."

"Your father-"

I touch my cheek gingerly, and wince. "I'll deal with him. I'm sleeping in. So should you."

"Yes, Ma'am."

She rises, and most of the sandwich goes in the garbage. As she's leaving, I sigh.

"Alicia."

"Yes?"

"For what's worth, *I* don't hate *you*."

A little while later I add, "I just hate myself," but by then I'm alone again.

Chapter Five

Victor

Fuck fuck fuck, fuck me sideways with a blowtorch.

First thing I do is push past some asshole in a paisley tie (really?) and into the men's room. I shoulder my way into a toilet stall. I don't want to touch anything. Then I slip my fingers in my mouth. I can still taste her on my fingers. The stall rattles when I slam my fist into the wall. My hand comes away bloody, a spider-web crack in the tile. Shit.

Shit, shit, shit, shit, *shit*.

She did not say 'don't leave me'. That was just my imagination. I'm sure of it.

I walk out of the bathroom with a bloodied hand and paisley tie man is waiting for me. He gives my hand a look and I realize I'm being sized up.

Look, I don't pretend to be the hardest hardass that was ever hard, but you learn things in prison. Rule number one, is don't go around sizing people up. Paisley tie man, besides having

70

atrocious taste, is ex military. Still wears a crew-cut and lifts three times a week. He commutes into the city and has a room full of gun parts and Army manuals he bought from a surplus catalog, stuff about close combat techniques and booby traps. I can see all that written on his face, somehow.

You get good at reading faces in jail.

"Hey," he snaps at me.

This guy pilots a desk at the biscuit factory headquarters. I'm not in the fucking mood. I walk past him to the sink and wash my hands. I've got my blood from the broken tile on my right and Eve's pussy juice on my left. The water goes down the sink pink. The paper towel sticks to my hand. I like this bathroom, it reminds me of a casino. It would be a terrible shame if one of those nice porcelain urinals was cracked in half by this asshole's head. The probability of that is rising by the second.

I pull the paper towel away. A few little nicks, nothing serious. I squeeze the paper against the blood and take a deep breath. Count to ten. Conflict management was something else I had to learn. After sitting through enough bullshit

71

anger management sessions I actually started paying attention and *sharing* in hopes they'd stop making me go.

I told them some shit about being angry that my Dad died. I'm not angry with him. It's not Dad's fault some asshole ran him off the road into a tree. What makes me angry is that I gave myself completely to Eve and at the first sign of trouble she believed the absolute worst about me. I can still see her father's smug face behind her as she reacted to the bitch's testimony at the trial. Martin. The man has the most punchable face. I wouldn't mind hammering him with my fist. Paisley tie man hasn't given up volunteering to stand in for Martin today. He's edging closer to me all the time as I pat my hand dry again, run more water over it. The cuts are already starting to scab. He looks in the toilet stall and then back at me.

"Did you do that?"

"Not now."

I start walking away.

"I asked you a fucking question."

He puts his hand on me.

Oh, fuck you.

I duck from under his grip as he paws at my suit coat. Turn, pivot on my heels, and suddenly his fingers are crushed in my grip. A twist and a squeeze and they'll pop right out of joint, or I can spin on my heel and hammer my elbow against his, snap it clean. I could totally fuck him up, but I stop. I let go. He goes for me again, grabs at my collar with both hands. I slip my arms up between his and spread them apart, breaking his grip. If I hit this guy, I'm going back to prison.

The bathroom door bangs open and Jim Thorpe III walks in.

III. Part of his name is a goddamn Roman numeral. What am I doing here?

"Howard? What the fuck are you doing?"

Howard the Paisley Tie man blinks. Looks at me. Blinks again. He walks off muttering, leaving me to adjust my collar and coat gingerly, trying not to get blood on my fingers.

When we're alone, Thorpe walks over.

"What the hell is going on?"

"Don't worry about it."

"You have a history with that woman, I take it. It's not just a business thing."

"No, it isn't. It's also none of your business. Let it lay."

"Right. The board has decided to take a formal vote from the shareholders. It's going to be a proxy fight. That woman has a few big proxies in her pocket already."

Like I give a shit.

"Give me names and numbers. I'll handle it."

"I'm in debt up to my eyeballs, Amsel. If she takes over the company, I'm fucked. Do you understand me? I'm not talking credit unions here. I mean leg breakers."

I shrug. "I'm not the one who bet on those basketball games, Thorpe. I know exactly who you're in debt to. I said I'll take care of it. Eve isn't getting shit from you."

He eyes me coldly, nods twice.

"Go bang a secretary, Thorpe. Go two at a time, I don't care. I'll make the calls. Everything is going to be just fine."

With a hard look, he turns and departs. I'm alone in the bathroom and let out a long, deep breath that threatens to turn into a scream. I do not need this pressure right now. I scrub my fingers through my hair, make myself mostly presentable in the mirror and jog to the elevator, too late realizing I might run into Eve. The temptation to just throw her over my shoulder, tie her to a chair and *make* her listen to me would be too strong to resist.

You know what? There's more prayer in prison than a church. People pray, they pray a lot. Save me, help me, forgive me. My prayer was never said out loud. Back when I was a kid and my father was still alive, we used to watch Cecil B. DeMille's *The Ten Commandments* with Charlton Heston at least once a month. Me and him in the big home theater. He could recite all the lines by memory. It was so weird. I mean it's a four hour movie, and any time something remotely related would come up in conversation he could start spewing lines from that movie like it was nothing. I never knew how he remembered all that. One line from the movie still sticks in my head. I guess it's a line from the Bible, actually. *And once more, Pharoah's heart was hardened.*

That was my prayer. I never said it out loud, not once. Please. Soften her heart again. Help her believe me.

I didn't fuck that girl, Eve. I didn't betray you. All I ever wanted was you. Nothing else matters.

The elevator doors open. There's a driver waiting for me. A narrow man with thinning hair he grows to his shoulders and a pinched, weasely face. I don't know his name and I don't care to ask. He doesn't talk.

My associates are not nice people. I prefer not to talk to them. I ride in the back of the car to the airport, to the private jet waiting for me. I don't know Eve's exact itinerary, but we'll be in the air at the same time, land around the same time. Finding her would be trivial, following her would be trivial. As I sit in the plush seat at the back of the plane and lean back into it, all I can think about is the warmth of her body under my hands, pressed against me, the urgency of her pumping hips as I thrust my fingers inside her. It's been so long.

Before Eve I could have any girl I wanted, and I did. Often.

Then there was Eve and all of a sudden there were two girls in the world. Her, and everyone else.

I'm not a big sleeper. Never had been. I used to vex my parents by lying awake until past midnight and rising with the sun. Even in high school when I was supposed to sleep in I rarely slept more than six or seven hours. There was just too much in the world to be awake for. Now all I want is a damned nap. A nap and Eve in a bed beside me, curled up the way she does when she sleeps, arms around me, pressed against my back. The plane seat is warm and soft but a poor substitute. Can't sleep through takeoff, but once the plane is in the air I do nod off. Adrenaline will do that to you. It's a crash worse than caffeine, just like the high is more intense. I nod off into a dreamless and not very restful sleep and when I wake again, the plane is leaning back into the landing. It's always struck me as strange how planes tilt *backwards* when they're going to land, but I guess it makes sense.

The landing is gentle, at least. I want off this fucking thing. Best thing about private planes is no waiting around for all the nonsense. I'm down the steps and walking across tarmac in less than ten minutes after landing.

I stumble to a stop when I spot my jet. Well, the Amsel holding company's jet. Eve is there. I can't see her. I don't have to. I can feel her.

Time to go, before I do something stupid like throw myself at her feet and tell her everything.

Usually, when one flies on a private jet, one does not take the bus. Yet I walk through the terminal and catch the bus out to the short term parking lot. The Firebird is parked way off on its own, a long walk from where the bus lets me off. I've seen some shit, but the way the high pressure sodium lamps that illuminate the parking lot leech all the color out of the world is fucking eerie, especially on a moonless, cloudy night. It's going to rain again, or maybe snow. It's colder now than it was this morning. I feel like I've been awake for three days. I slip into the car and lean on the steering wheel, resting my forehead on the cold metal. I give the key a twist and she starts right up. I need to find the time to get under the hood and check her out, sometime. She probably needs an oil change. Dad would flip out if he knew I just drove her off after sitting for years without a thorough going over.

When I sit up and lean back in the seat the last thing I want to do is drive. Fortunately I don't have far to go. It's a short hop into the city, off the highway and back to the parking lot. The bleary-eyed attendant eyes the Firebird warily as I take my ticket and park it. I should probably buy a monthly pass but I'm not putting a sticker on my car. I stick it in my pocket and walk across the street without bothering to look and see if a car is coming, then head up the stairs. I stumble into the dingy little room, slam the door and twist the lock. I don't bother with the stupid little chain. I kick my shoes into the corner, slough off my clothes like dead skin and flop onto the mattress, then paw around until I come up with about a third of a bottle of Jack. I drink it like it's water, feel the heat spread through me and hope it'll dull my senses a little, but it doesn't.

I drink the rest, too fast. Toss the bottle and it thunks in the corner, clinks against another one. There's a pile of them over there I haven't bothered to clean up.

I roll over on my side, and try to sleep.

The mattress is too damned soft. I end up shimmying off of it, onto the floor, grab my bare pillow and tuck it under my head. The hard floor is better, easier to sleep on. My back will be killing me in the morning, but at least I can sleep.

Somebody flips a switch and suddenly there's sunlight pouring through the windows and it feels like my head is stuffed with pencil erasers. I roll away from the bed onto my hands, get my feet under me and start push-ups. It only makes my head throb more, but I do a hundred in quick succession. If I wasn't so fatigued last night I'd be clapping with every rep. Get up, grab the pull up bar I've bolted to the wall, and start counting, stop counting when I get bored with it and go until my arms and back are on fire. If my head hurt any worse I'd be dead. I look in the small, grimy mirror in the tiny bathroom to make sure there's no blood squirting out my nose, limp over to the fridge and pull out the bottle of milk inside. I down a cocktail of sinus pills, aspirin, Excedrin, and ibuprofen, wash it down with gulps of milk, eat some cold Pop Tarts and fall back down on the bed.

I sit there for a couple hours, clutching my head. When the pain has faded to merely excruciating, I'm ready to get up and get to work. Clean clothes first, and then the office.

My phone buzzes. I rifle through my shed suit to find it and press it to my ear.

"What?" I snap, yawning.

"Victor. Is that any way to greet your old friend?"

Fuck. It's Vitali.

Vitali the Hammer.

"Sorry, Vitali. What is it?"

"Early day, yes? How did meeting go yesterday?"

He slips into a Russian accent now and then. It's weird, jarring when he does it. He does it when he's upset. He likes asking people questions he already knows the answer to, to test them. I don't like being tested.

"As expected."

"How did the girl take it?"

"That's not your problem. Thorpe is squarely on my side. It's coming down to a proxy fight. She'll lose."

"Yes, you said it would. Give me the names of the holdouts."

I swallow. "Let me call them first."

"As you wish. Call me this afternoon and tell me you have succeeded, or give me the names of the holdouts."

He hangs up. Vitali is only a man for niceties when it suits him, which is mostly when he thinks it's funny.

They call him the hammer for a reason. He once told me a man's toes look like grapes after you take a masonry hammer to them.

What have I gotten myself into?

Worse, what have I gotten Eve into?

Before I agreed to any of this I extracted a promise from Vitali that Eve would not be hurt.

Then again, it wasn't much of a promise, and I didn't extract it, exactly. When somebody like Vitali promises somebody won't be hurt, it's like when they come around and promise your shop won't burn down if you pay in the insurance money. That kind of a promise.

I'll keep her safe, I swear.

I start by calling a dozen old men and begging, pleading, arguing, joking my way through to thwarting Eve's attempts to bring the biscuit company under the Amsel umbrella, and when that doesn't work, lay down a few veiled threats.

When I call Vitali to tell him it's a go, I make the conversation as brief as possible. He hangs up on me again.

Dick.

I guess I should be proud of myself. I saved Jim Thorpe's company from Eve's claws. I sold them to the Russian Mafia instead. Russian Mafia biscuits. I hope they don't start putting ground up witnesses in the batter or something. With that done I flop back on the bed.

Air. I need air. It stinks in here. Opening the windows won't help, it just makes the smell worse. I dress quickly and duck out of the apartment, walk down the street with my hands shoved in my pockets. Two stores down the block there's a bar. Bad idea. Me plus booze plus crowd equals fight, equals parole violation, equals back to the cell. I walk to the corner and just stand there, ignoring the walk/don't walk signal. If I stand too long some cop will roll up and ask what I'm doing, so I keep moving.

Across Market Street and up 4th. I'm heading in a bad direction. I turn around, start back. The air out here isn't any better. It's cold today, colder than yesterday and there's a breeze off the river, with all the lovely smells you'd expect. I make sure to wait for the signals before I cross, stay in the crosswalk, keep my head down. Last thing I need is to eyefuck some stranger into a fistfight.

As I start up the rickety cast iron stairs to my so-called apartment, I hear shouting, some in English, some in Korean, and a thump, and a scream.

It's coming from my downstairs neighbors.

A louder scream.

Oh God damn it.

I've never been in one of these places before. The only signage is a red paper lantern hanging by the door, a pretty universal signal. It's a red light. Yeah.

Inside the first door there's another, locked. I hear more commotion and ring the doorbell.

No answer.

Turn around, Victor. It's not your problem. Leave it be.

There's a deadbolt. It gives under one blow from my shoulder, rips the strike plate out of the wall with a shower of splinters. I hear the sound of a fist on flesh and rush towards it.

Inside is chaos. I've never been in here before, never had any interest. It's a maze, a bunch of rooms off a twisting hallway. A half-naked *masseuse* wearing nothing but a bright blue thong and one high heeled shoe runs past me, away from the noise.

Then a short Korean woman with a shocked expression comes tumbling through a door, wide-eyed. She lands on her ass and grunts in Korean, then starts shouting. I walk down the hall towards her, and out comes a pretty good sized, middle aged man, dragging a tiny slip of a girl by the arm. She's completely buck-ass nude, and in other circumstances I'd been getting quite a show, but her nakedness is just shameful. There's a bruise on her cheek.

Bad move, big man.

"Finish!" the girl screams, in broken English. "Hour done! Hour done!"

She pulls at his fingers and pounds his arm with her fist, and I realize he's dragging her *back* into the room.

Oh Jesus.

"*Hey,*" I bark out, so loud it rattles the ceiling. "Party's over, handsome. Get your fucking hand off the girl."

The woman looks at me. The girl looks at me.

The big guy looks at me.

"You think you're a big man, don't you? You want to go? Let's go."

It all happens at once. He shoves the girl. She's still got her fucking heels on. Time slows, that way it does, like in a car accident. You learn to keep your head on a swivel where I've been. When I see the girl's ankle fold under her as she goes down, it's like something cracks in my chest and scalding, molten fury burns in my lungs.

The big man's fist hits my chin. He's fast. He's good.

I fight dirty. I roll with the blow, turn, pivot, and lash out with my foot. I take him in the side of his leg, the knee. It knocks him off balance, and I bring my shin up between his legs, a savage kick that crushes his balls and sends him back, howling. He's forgotten about me.

I'm not done.

My fist hammers into his nose. I feel it fold under my hand, feel the snap and the spray of blood. I get him by the hair, grabbing a handful right above his forehead, turn, and pull. He claws at my hand, but I'm not pulling his hair. I let go and he goes face first into the wall. This an old building. Plaster walls as hard as stone. A lot harder than his face. He bounces back, flails, and starts to grapple with me, but there's blood in his eyes. I feel something pop in my hand as I hit him right in the cheekbone, but something in his head pops from the blow, too. He slams against the other wall and goes down, grabbing at my legs. His arms wrap around my legs and I go down with him, hit the floor hard. The world flashes when the back of my head hits the hardwood floor. Then a first hits my jaw, and the world starts spinning.

Hands yank me up by the collar of my shirt. It rips, but not enough. Then a white flash as my head hits the floor. A fist raises over my head, ready to come down.

When your head is braced against something rigid, that's a bad way to get hit. I jerk out of the way at the last second, and he howls as his fist hits the hardwood. Then I knee him in the stomach, grab his throat, and kick him in the balls again. His howl comes out choked, and he claws at my wrists, but I'm stronger. I feel his grip weakening.

A shadow falls over me and there is a tremendous *clang*.

Big man rolls off of me onto the floor, a bloody gash on his head. The woman hit him with a fucking frying pan.

"Police come," she says, offering me a hand. "You go. Out the back."

I'm not arguing. I limp along with her past a half dozen girls in states of dress varying from "string covering clit" to pajamas and one wearing a goddamn chef toque (am I dreaming this?) and out the back. Christ, if somebody sees me I'm fucked. I run back around to the side and lurch up the stairs, through my door and fall to my knees on the floor.

My fucking head. Figures I'm out of booze.

Half an hour later I get up. It's daylight outside but it's overcast now, enough for the red and blues to flash in my window. Quickly I discard my clothes. My t-shirt is bloody, and I'm not sure if it's mine or not. I get all my clothes off, shove them in a trash bag and frantically dart around the room, naked. If the cops come banging on my door asking questions and see something incriminating they'll bust in and I'll be on a bus back to prison by dark. Once I'm reasonably certain there's nothing poking out that would catch their attention, I get under scalding hot water in the shower.

"Fuck," I grunt.

A fight just makes me feel more alive. Feeling more alive makes me want Eve that much more. I rest my head on the grimy tiles and run the water until it goes cold.

Chapter Six

Evelyn

My assistant finds me at my desk, slumped and leaning on my hand. She stops in the door and flinches when she lays eyes on me.

I know why. At this point I'm using my computer screen for a mirror more than anything else. My hair is a tousled mess, my eyes are bloodshot, there is an ugly bruise on my face and I look like I haven't slept, because I didn't. I laid awake all night staring at the ceiling, and my eyes are red from crying, livid lines running down my cheeks like claw marks. Even my unbruised cheek is puffy, and there's a fine crust of blood around the nostril on the side where he hit me. A cup of cold coffee sits next to me on the desk, glued to the wood by a drying brown ring. An untouched bagel rests beside it, the cream cheese still sealed in the little cup. I take one look at Alicia and look back down at the desk.

"Go home," I murmur. "I can't work like this."

She closes the door and sits in the chair in front of my desk.

"Miss Ross," she starts.

"Eve," I correct. "Call me Eve. My name is Eve."

"Eve," she says, rolling the syllable around her mouth like an unfamiliar taste. "Eve, I was talking to my husband last night. We think you should call the police."

I sigh softly. "About what?"

She touches her cheek.

"What are the police going to do for me?" I say.

"Honey, you can't let him hurt you like this."

I blink a few times. She sounds like a mother.

Makes me wonder what my mother sounded like. I stifle a little noise that's almost a sob, fold my arms on the desk and plunge my face into them. Then the sobbing starts. I'm still in my pajamas, plain powder blue terrycloth. Victor bought them for me. The blue brings out my eyes, he said.

The longer I sit there the harder I sob. I don't care if Alicia sees me crying anymore.

Gingerly, she rests her hand on my back, behind my neck, and rubs.

"Hey. Hey. Here."

I sit up and she hands me a box of tissues. I snatch a handful of them and scrub at my face, and wince when I touch the bruise. It still hurts. I need to cover it, but I don't much experience with makeup. I could drape some hair over that side of my face, I suppose. I used to wear it that way when I was younger, when I first started school. I was so afraid of my tutors.

I continue to stare dully at nothing as Alicia drags her chair around to my side of the desk, and sits next to me. I can't bring myself to look at her. I just sniff, whimper and stare at my desk. She takes the uneaten food and sticky coffee cup, wipes the desk and carries it all away. A few minutes later she returns with a yogurt cup and a can of Coke. I look at them with disdain, and she simply ignores me, pops the top of the can and peels back the yogurt lid, and sticks a spoon in it.

Then she sets it before me like she expects me to eat it.

Grudgingly, I pick it up and cradle it in my hand, and take a small bit from the tip of the spoon. I choke down a half-chewed, half-frozen blueberry and feel like I'm going to puke.

"You need to eat," she says, firmly.

Every bite is an effort. I hate yogurt anyway, but something about her folded arms and unyielding stare makes me eat it, then sip at the soda. I have no idea why she thinks this garbage is healthy, but it works. I feel just a bit better when I'm finished.

She sinks into the chair next to me. I sit back in my chair and look up at the ceiling.

"Tell me, whatever it is."

"You've lost Thorpe," she says, her voice flat. "They signed on with… with Victor."

I nod slowly.

"I see."

"I haven't heard from your father."

I flinch when she says it.

"Eve," she says.

I shake my head, slowly.

"There's nowhere I can go. Nowhere I can run. I can't get away from him. Only one person could ever protect me from him and he…" I suck in a breath, and go rigid.

"Yesterday," Alicia says, slowly. "When you were alone in that room with him."

"With Victor."

"Did he… did he force," she swallows, hard. "Did he do something to you?"

The sides of my mouth curl in a small, secret smile. "Nothing I didn't want him to do. He never would."

"You're in love with him."

She has a way of stating questions so they come out as statements, this woman does. It hurts, to be seen through so clearly. I can't look at her.

"He didn't seem so terrible. What did he do?"

I clutch my hand over my mouth, press my eyes shut and suppress a full body shudder.

"I gave him everything," I choke out, "and he threw me away like I was trash."

She blinks a few times, and cocks her head to the side. "I thought… I was under the impression he was your stepbrother."

"He was. Is. Is he still my stepbrother if his mother is dead? I don't even know. It wasn't like that. We first met when I was eighteen. I'd just finished high school."

"How did you meet?"

"My father was dating his mother. When it got serious he brought me to meet her. He was here, of course. It's his house."

Not was. Is.

This is not my place. I wish I knew where my place was.

"That sounds like a cute way to meet."

"Our parents got married."

"So? It's not as if you grew up together."

I sigh, long and loud. "I've heard that before."

"From him," she says.

"Yes."

"I'm here if you want to tell me. I'll listen."

I look at her. I look around the office.

"Morning report?"

"You have three-hundred and seventy two emails, six calls, four requests for meetings, the Wall Street Journal wants an interview, TMZ wants a comment on..."

"Nevermind. Wait, TMZ?"

"Your, ah, encounter yesterday is all over Twitter."

"*Twitter?* Who the hell on Twitter cares about what I do?"

"Lots of people, apparently. You do realize you're famous, right?"

"I am?"

She sighs. "Sweetheart, you're the tenth richest woman in the world."

"Ninth," I correct.

"Tenth," she insists. "I hadn't gotten to the stock dip yet."

I sit up. "Stock dip?"

"Your net worth decreased by two-hundred and fifty-six million dollars yesterday afternoon. It's still going down."

She looks at me like she expects me to start screaming, but the number is unreal. Does it even matter? When you have billions, plural, does any amount of money matter? I've never wanted for anything in my entire life. I'm such a bitch, worried about things like this when people are...

"How much are you paid?"

"Forty-two five, plus benefits."

I blink a few times. I have *things* that cost more than she makes in a year. Things I don't even want or bother with. I swallow a lump in my throat but it won't go down.

96

"Check the indexes again."

She sighs and opens her laptop, frowns as she reads the reports.

"Eleventh richest woman. The stock is tanking, Eve. I'm sorry."

"Why?"

"Why is it tanking? Presumably because this is the first time-"

"No, why are you sorry? I'll earn more in interest today than you'll make in your entire life."

She scowls at me.

"I didn't mean it like that."

"What did you mean?"

I plunge my face in my folded arms again.

"I wish I could just disappear."

Her hand settles on my back. Why is she being kind to me? What did I ever do for her?

"You know, they say money can't buy happiness."

I snort. "They say lots of things. I've never seen it buy anybody sadness."

She's quiet for a while.

"I think I have."

I sit up but I can't bring myself to look at her.
I jiggle the mouse and stare through the
computer screen. It's too fuzzy to read, but the
blur is from tears. I sniff again and Alicia passes
me a tissue without comment. My nose is raw
but I scrub at it anyway. I should do some work.
I can answer emails at least.

Trembling, I reach for the keyboard.

"You can't work like this."

"If I don't, Father will be upset."

"He'll hit you again?"

I touch my cheek and wince. "He forgot
himself. He hasn't done that since I was-"

She cuts me off. "He shouldn't *ever* do that.
Not leave a mark like that. When was the last
time?"

I swallow, hard. "I was in high school."

"You were an *adult?*" she says, wide-eyed.
"When was the last time before *that?*"

"Not often when I was a teenager. More
frequently when I was smaller. He used to use
his belt."

Alicia stares at me, open-mouthed.

"Did your step-family know about this?"

"Not at first," I murmur.

"You can talk to me."

I look over at her.

"Do you understand what you're risking by approaching me this way? If my father finds out I've been talking to you about any of this, you could be ruined. Permanently. Your husband, too."

"Is he going to find out?"

"Not from me."

I open my email client and type up a quick email to human resources. Quick and to the point.

"What was that?"

"I just tripled your salary."

"Are you going to send Tiny Tim a goose now?"

I snort, and then break out laughing. Oh God, I haven't laughed in years. Alicia stares at me.

"Oh my God. I'm She-Scrooge." My laughter quickly melts into sobs again. "How did this happen to me? I don't want to be this way."

"What way to you want to be?"

"What are you, my therapist now?"

"No, but I have three girls. The oldest is in college. I've seen worse than this."

I blink at her a few times. "Really?"

"A sixteen year old's boyfriend freakout is a force of nature."

"I never had a boyfriend until I was… older than that."

"Your stepbrother."

"Yes."

She shifts in her seat and shrugs. "You want to tell me about it."

"Stop saying questions like they're statements."

"That was a statement," she sighs. "You do want to talk, you're just trying to find the words."

"I haven't had a real conversation with another human being about anything but my work in five years."

"I can tell," Alicia says, dryly.

I give her a look.

"My daughter looks at me like that when I say something she knows is right."

I look at the computer again. I have more emails.

An urge strikes me. I open the browser, navigate to Twitter and type my name in the search box.

I suck in a deep breath when I read what I see. There must be thousands of tweets. I glance at Alicia and bite my lip, and scroll through the screen.

There's a hashtag.

"I have a hashtag," I blurt out.

#EveDestroyedMyLife

Trembling, I click the link.

For the next twenty minutes, I sit in silence and read, my face a still mask. The tweets go on forever. This only started yesterday.

I had 19 years of seniority and a pension. #EveRuinedMyLife

I snap the computer's screen down and stare at the door, trembling. Then I get up.

"I need to get out of here."

"You're in your pajamas."

I look down at myself.

"Go take a shower and change."

I am not used to be ordered around, at least by anyone but my father, but I do as she says. My shower turns out to be half an hour standing under the hot water followed by brushing my hair and dressing in the only casual clothes I have, an ancient sweatsuit at the bottom of my bottom drawer, which I don't remember even putting there. I don't have sneakers, either. I don't care; I put on a pair of slippers and make a mental note to buy some sneakers. When I step outside, Alicia is waiting for me.

"Should I have the car brought around?"

"Do you have a car?"

She nods.

"Let's take yours."

I feel strange walking out of the house, down the path that winds around the back to where Alicia and the other staff park. Her car is a boxy minivan. The inside smells strongly of fabric softener for some reason. I sit in the front seat next to her, and she starts the engine and looks over at me.

"Where would we be going, then?"

I sigh. "I want a cheeseburger."

"What kind?"

"I don't know. Pick one."

Some twenty minutes later, I find myself sitting in her minivan while she wheels it around the curving drive-through lane of a McDonalds. She stops before pulling up to the speaker.

"What did you want, hon?"

"A quarter pounder."

She orders, pulls up, and I realize I have no cash on me. My God, I'm making her pay.

"I'll pay you back," I say, as she pulls into a parking space facing the road.

She passes me my food and I spread the paper open on my lap.

"You don't have to pay me back. It was nine dollars."

I peel the top of the bun off and use a napkin to wipe it clean, leaving a thin layer of mayonnaise-ketchup-mustard mixture soaked into the bread, then settle it on top of the patty and take a bite.

"If you'd said something I'd have ordered it plain for you."

"I like it this way."

She eyes me while she chews. "You mean you like to order it and then peel everything off."

"Yes. They just put too much on."

"Okay."

Every bite is like torture. The food is fine, the memories are not. It's like every bite tries to stick in my throat.

"Evelyn," she says.

I put the half-eaten burger on the paper in my lap and thoroughly clean my hands with a pale yellow napkin. I fold the burger in the paper and stick it back in the bag, and take a long pull on the soda she bought me.

"Thank you for lunch," I say, barely more than a whisper.

Alicia says nothing else until she balls up the wrapper from her fish sandwich and tosses it in the open bag. She reaches for the key, to start the van.

"Wait."

Her hand sinks back to her lap. I stare straight ahead.

"This is what happened."

Chapter Seven

Evelyn

Mrs. Vanderburg placed the folder in my hands.

"You've done very well, Eve."

My face lit up in a smile so hard it hurt. This was a strange week. I was saying goodbye to my tutors. A dozen admission letters rested in two neat stacks on my desk, behind Mrs. V. Of all my teachers, she was the one I loved most. For the last four years, all through high school, she visited three times per week to instruct me in mathematics. I missed a few points on the papers she handed back, but I didn't care. I was excited and full of fear at the same time, my stomach doing backflips.

Today I would be saying goodbye to a fixture in my life. When you are eighteen years old, four years is a long time. In all those years of instruction, I'd never seen Mrs. V wear anything but an ankle length dress, usually buttoned to her neck. She looked like she belonged in a Victorian period piece, except for her big oversized glasses, more practical than stylish. In the years I'd known her, half-moon shaped bifocal lenses had appeared in those glasses, and her tightly wound bun went from silver to mostly white.

I almost didn't bother looking at the papers. It was a foregone conclusion at this point. The paperwork had been filed, and I had my diploma, the equivalent of an honors track diploma at a regular high school. Deep down I've always suspected that *every* homeschooled student earns a perfect grade point average, but I know I earned it.

"Have you decided where you'll be going?"

I blinked a few times and glanced at the letters.

"I'm not sure yet." My voice was tiny then, soft, barely more than a whisper.

"You have quite a selection to choose from." The note of approval in her voice makes my pride swell.

She took my hands, and cleared her throat, but she was becoming choked up. I felt my eyes burn in return.

"Students like you are the reason I wanted to become a teacher," she told me, with a wistful sigh. "I worry about you, though."

"Why? Did I do something wrong?"

She smiles and pats my hand. "No, sweet girl. You did nothing wrong. You are a kind, sensitive, well mannered young woman and you are very intelligent, and, if I may say so, quite beautiful. Just look at you blush."

I was blushing.

"Be very careful," she said, a note of warning in her voice. "You're very trusting. Soon you'll be on your own, with no one there to look out for you but yourself. You have to be very careful, especially about young men."

I nodded. "I know. F-father talked to me about this."

She let out a long sigh, released my hands and folded her own in her lap.

"Eve, normally I would not say this, but what will he do, hmm? Fire me? Your father is not always right. I want you to be cautious. He wants to control every aspect of your life. In truth, I think you'd have prospered in traditional school. A private institution, perhaps. You are very intelligent and learn quickly, but there are some lessons only people your own age can teach you, and you've been deprived of them. I don't know why."

She cleared her throat.

"I'd ask you not to repeat any of this. I depend on recommendations in my line of work, you understand."

I nod. "Of course, I'll keep anything you say in confidence."

"'Be careful' doesn't mean 'stay away from every boy'. You're intelligent. Use that intelligence. Trust your instincts. Avoid situations where you can be taken advantage of. Promise me, though, that you won't shut people out. Make some friends. It may take you a while to learn how. Don't wall yourself off. A life lived alone is not a good life."

I nodded again. "Thank you, Mrs. V."

She scrubbed at her eyes with her fingers.

"You know, I have to leave now."

"You could stay for dinner."

"I don't think your father would like that, dear. No," she sighed again, and I realized she was beginning to choke up. "I need to go. I have an appointment this afternoon, anyway."

I stood up and walked her to the front door of our house. At the door, she shocked me by throwing her arms around me. She hugged me. I stood there rigid, unsure what I should do. She held me by the shoulders and gave me warm smile.

"Remember what I said. It's time to leave the nest."

"Thank you," I said, not sure what else to say.

There was an awkward pause, and with a hitching breath she descended the front steps and walked down the street to her car. I waved as she drove off, and felt a crushing weight in the pit of my stomach as I walked back to the study that served as my classroom. My next tutor taught history and English and we were not so close. Our final interaction was professional, the advice given more about choosing a field of study. I had already chosen. I would be studying business. Tonight, when Father came home, I was expected to inform him which school I would attend, and begin making the arrangements. After the history tutor left, I sat at the desk and arranged the envelopes into piles. I was tempted to choose a college in Oregon, as far from home as I could get, but the idea of being so far away made my fingers tremble and my palms sweaty. It went in the No pile. I don't even know why I applied.

I don't know why I applied to any of them. The envelope sat fat in front of me, heavy with the future. I was offered a full scholarship, not that we needed it.

When Father came home I was waiting for him in the hallway. It was the same, every day. I lurked near the door, walked over as he entered and took his briefcase, and told him about my studies for the day as I walked with him to his office. Once inside I set his briefcase by the desk. He sat down behind the broad expanse of oak and bored into me with his icy blue eyes.

"Well?"

I did my trick. It's a clever trick.

I opened my mouth and his words came out.

"A good choice," was all he said. "You're excused. Dinner is at six thirty."

Father employed a domestic to cook and clean for us. Most never lasted more than six months.

Imelda, the latest, had been there for nine. She was quiet, only a few years older than I was, and had a way of looking through me as if I was not there. I ate my serving of steamed vegetables and lemon pepper chicken slowly, cutting neatly, taking small bites.

Dinner conversation was never our strong suit.

"Tomorrow afternoon, you will come with me."

"Yes, sir."

I didn't ask where. It wasn't my place.

"We'll be visiting Karen Amsel."

"One of your clients."

"She's more than a client."

My stomach twisted. I looked at a bite of perfectly grilled chicken stuck on the tines of my fork and resisted the urge to put it down. I needed to clean my plate.

Girls are supposed to have opinions about their fathers dating. I wasn't sure what I thought about it. I knew he'd been spending a great deal of time with her for the last several months. He'd been eating with her, but I assumed he was simply working late. My father was a financial advisor, working with any number of high profile clients. Mrs. Amsel was among the richest. I'd never met her. He wasn't one to show me off to the clients. When they came to the house, either on business or for a social call, I was told to stay in my bedroom. Mrs. Amsel had never paid a call, socially or professionally.

"We've discussed marriage."

"I see."

"I expect you to be on your best behavior."

"Yes, sir."

"You're excused, when you finish."

Picking at the vegetables took longer, but I finally finished and took our plates back to the kitchen. Imelda had gone home. She would wash up in the morning. I stacked them neatly in the sink, returned to make sure my chair was neatly pushed in, and left. Father paid me no mind, reading the *Wall Street Journal* as he sipped his evening coffee.

I retreated to my bedroom. I wasn't allowed to use the Internet except for school and television was also forbidden. After my evening shower, I settled into bed with a book. I had a box of romance novels tucked under my bed.

One of my tutors gave them to me when I asked her about them. I'd read them all five times and half of them were on the verge of losing pages, but I carefully repaired them with tape and glue. Tonight, though, I leaned back and read one of the books I was actually allowed to purchase on our last trip to the store.

By nine o'clock I was in bed, dead tired from rising at five. Tomorrow would be a strange day, only a little stranger than all the rest of the days until I started whatever advanced reading I needed for my college courses. I wouldn't have anything to *do*. I'd never had that much leisure time in my life. For as long as I could remember, my studies continued during the summer.

The next morning I put my responses to my acceptance letters in the mailbox. I'd scheduled a tour for July and I would be receiving my orientation paperwork soon. I was almost giddy at the thought, biting my lip in excitement.

I dressed in a light blue sun dress for the... date? Meeting? Was I being presented? I wasn't sure what to call it, or what it would be like. What if this woman disliked me? I'd be out of the house, soon.

It was a long drive from the city to our destination. I was wide-eyed the whole way, my hands folded neatly in my lap. My heart was pounding when Father turned off the road and drove through a huge wrought iron gate, down a stone path towards the biggest house I had ever seen. It looked like a haunted mansion in a movie, not that I'd seen that many. Two wings curling in a huge U-shape, each two floors jutting out from the three story house. It was topped by a cupola and all brick, covered mostly in ivy. Father parked under a tall portico and handed off his keys to a valet, I suppose he was. After Father let me out, the man drove off in our car, to park it somewhere. He put on a smile and touched my shoulder and led me up a wide, tall set of marble stairs to the broad front door of the house. A serving man in white pulled it open from inside.

Mrs. Amsel was younger than my father, short and plump and pretty, with a warm smile and riglets of thick brown hair that she'd tied back behind her neck. When he walked in she rushed over, touched his arms and kissed him. I looked away, feeling my cheeks burn. Father disliked public displays of affection, but I supposed this wasn't really public, after all. She turned to me.

"You must be Eve. Martin told me so much about you."

"Yes. It's a pleasure to meet you…"

"Karen," she finished. "Are you hungry?"

"Yes, I am. Thank you," I added quickly.

"We'll be eating out on the terrace."

"Where's Victor?" said Father.

Karen sucked in a breath. "He's around. I told him when I expected you."

Father smiled at her, but his eyes were hard.

Just then I heard the soft thud of bare feet on carpet and looked up.

A sweeping grand staircase lofted to the second floor, and currently descending it was a young man a year older than I was, tall and lean, muscled like a swimmer or a champion weightlifter. He was shirtless and barefoot and I don't think he had anything on under his jeans, either. They were very low on his waist. I stared at him. He looked like one of the models on the cover of the books my old tutor gave me. Except none of them had tattoos. He did. Feathers lined both of his arms, etched in black into his skin, sweeping over his shoulders to connect to a design on his back while an open mouthed, screaming raven spread across his chest. My eyes naturally followed the V-shape of his body, and I felt heat rising. He had veins bulging out even on his tightly muscled stomach, and v-channels of muscle along his sides that dove down into the waistband of his jeans. They looked like they'd slide down at any second.

He stepped off the stairs with a spring in his step.

"Victor," Karen said, dryly. "Shirt."

He looked down. "What? It's hot outside."

"I'm not amused," My father said, in an acid tone.

"It's not your house."

"Victor," Karen snapped. "Get dressed."

"Right, right. High tea with the Queen." He shot a look at my father.

Then he looked at me. It was like he'd only just noticed me. I expected him to look at me like some particularly curious and unwelcome species of insect, but he actually flinched when she set eyes on me.

Then he walked over.

"Well, hello," he said, smoothing his hair back with one hand while holding out the other.

"Victor!" his mother snapped.

"Aren't you going to introduce me?"

"Stop being such a barbarian."

He sighed.

"I'm Eve," I blurted out.

He looked at me without missing a beat. "So where's Adam?"

I should have said something, but all of a sudden my throat turned to sand. Everyone was looking at me.

Especially Victor. *Especially*.

"Get dressed," his mother growled.

"Fine," he sighed. "I'll be back in a minute."

He stopped halfway up the staircase, as Karen led us through the house.

"Hey, Eve!" he called.

"Yes?"

Father eyed me, his eyes like chips of cold blue stone.

"Want to go for a ride with me later?"

"A ride in what-"

"No," Father said, sharply. "She does not."

"I didn't ask you."

"Victor," his mother said, in a warning tone.

I heard his feet ascend the staircase as Karen led us through the house, towards the rear grounds. The *terrace* was bigger than a tennis court, a broad expanse of stone covered by a roof held up by heavy columns. There were four places set at a table, and despite the May heat there was a nice breeze blowing under the shadowy roof. It made me shiver as it raked across my shoulders. Father pulled out my chair for me. Victor did not appear, even after a servant brought tea sandwiches. Father chatted with Karen. I answered questions here or there when she asked me, but didn't dare interject. She kept eyeing me as I nibbled a very tasty tuna salad sandwich.

"May I be excused for a moment? I need to freshen up."

Karen smiled at me. "You don't need to be so formal, Eve. Sure, go ahead inside. If you see Victor tell him I said to get his butt out here."

Father shot me a look. I'm sure he appeared innocent enough to Karen but it made me flinch.

In no terms was I to repeat what she said in those exact words.

I quickly headed inside, slowing when I realized I had no idea where to find a powder room or guest bathroom or something like that. I thought I knew where the kitchen was. I could ask a member of the staff.

I turned the corner and almost walked into Victor. I skidded to a stop and stumbled, and rough hands closed around my arms. He steadied me, and quickly drew his hands away. It felt like my skin was burning where he touched me, and I knew I was as red as a beet.

"Oh. H-hello," I chirped.

"You okay?" he said, raising one eyebrow. "You look lost."

"I need to freshen up," I said.

He laughed. "You need to what? Seriously? You can drop that, there's nobody here but us."

I blinked a few times and looked away from him.

"I'm sorry."

I felt odd when he looked at me. He leaned on the wall and his gaze flicked downwards. My sun dress was modest but it stopped just below my

119

knees and I felt an itch on my legs. It was odd, though. I'd sensed men looking at me before, and been disgusted, but when he sized me up I almost felt flattered and, well, more. I had to look away as my cheeks and ears began burning.

"Okay. I'll show you where the bathroom is."

"Thank you."

"On one condition. You have to let me take you for a ride."

"On what?"

He snorted. "In my car, Eve. Can I call you Eve?"

"Yes-"

"Good, come on."

I wasn't sure what I just agreed to, but he turned on his heels and led me through the house to a door, and gestured grandly to it.

"The Pisser. All yours."

"You shouldn't talk like that."

"Why not?"

Oh. I didn't actually have a *reason*. It had just been drilled into me.

Whipped into me.

When I was done in the bathroom, he seized my wrist as I stepped out.

"Come on. Time to meet Charlene."

Chapter Eight

Evelyn

"I have to get back to lunch," I said, edging past him.

His hand shot out and closed, gently, around my wrist.

"Yeah, me too. Come on. We won't be long."

He tugged my arm but I held my ground, for a moment. I chanced to look at his eyes. I'd avoided them before. They were a piercing slate gray, and smiled more than his mouth did. Something fluttered in my chest, like I'd swallowed a moth, and I found my feet moving before I realized I was walking. His hand slipped from my wrist to cup around my fingers before letting go. The sun was warm outside. I saw the edge of the terrace, but we were out of sight from our parents as we emerged from a side door that opened onto a narrow path over to an old stables, converted into a garage with gleaming steel doors. Victor walked down the row and opened one of the bays with a flourish. He leaned on the door, arms over his head, and stretched. I licked my lips without knowing why as my eyes roamed down over his body. He was muscle all over, from head to toe, and his jeans and black t-shirt showed it magnificently.

After a glance over at me, he nodded at the car.

I didn't know cars, so to me it was just old and garish, a pearly white color with a huge multicolored decal of a fire breathing bird plastered across the hood. Victor rushed over to swing open the long passenger's door, and after a moment of lip chewing and look back at the house, I dropped inside. I shouldn't have been doing this, and I didn't know why I was. I glanced over and saw that Victor's door was locked, leaned over his seat and popped the button. He slipped into the seat and looked over at me with a secret smile on his face, like I passed some kind of test. I pulled my seatbelt on and locked my door. Victor did the same, shifted in the seat and stabbed in the clutch with his foot. When he turned the key I yelped and covered my ears. It was *loud*, like an old turboprop airplane. He revved the engine a few times and the noise increased.

I glanced over and saw Father and Mrs. Amsel running to the corner of the terrace. I couldn't make out their faces, we were too far away.

Victor laughed softly, put the car in gear and let out the clutch.

The force of the acceleration threw me back in the seat, and I screamed. The back end of the car swung around behind us and he opened the throttle, pushing me back into the seat again as the car pitched around the curved, narrow driveway, towards the front gate.

Victor slowed as the car rumbled out between the gates. As he did, he pulled something from his pocket. He slapped a one hundred dollar bill on the dashboard in front of me. A piece of tape held it in place.

"Hey," he said. "If you grab that, it's yours."

I blinked a few times. What was this, some kind of game? It was right there.

As I reached for it, he wheeled the car around and floored the accelerator. My fingers fell away from the dash as the acceleration crushed me into the seat. I screamed, out loud. If we went any faster I though the car would lift up into the air. I could actually see the front end rising. Victor laughed like a maniac, working through the gears with one hand, choking the wheel with the other, his hair blowing in the wind. The bill fluttered on the dashboard. I almost reached it when he shifted gears, but the sudden burst in speed sent me back into the seat. Then I found myself squeezing the bolsters at the sides as he took a curve in the road. He geared down and the car slowed, but I was too busy to grab for the bill. I thought for sure we would go flying off the road and slam into one of the trees that lined it. The tires screeched, and the car seemed to slide through the curve more than roll through it, until Victor turned the wheel sharply, cut through the oncoming lane and floored it, straightening out.

My heart pounded in my chest, my pulse throbbed behind my eyeballs, and I squeezed my legs together.

Every hill dropped the bottom out from under me, every curve sent a surge of naked fear through me, but Victor was in perfect control, his face a mask of concentration that only cracked with a smile in the straight stretches of road where he shot me a quick glance, studying me like I was some exotic creature.

Finally he slowed down on the road, and I noticed the ivy-lined wall flying past us. A wide swing to the right and he turned left across the road through the gates.

Our parents stood outside the stables. His mother had her arms crossed over her chest and a wry look on her face.

My father was as still as a statue, but purple with rage.

Victor pulled past the bay where he parked the car, swung around, and backed in. The sound of the motor grew to a teeth rattling rumble in the confined space before he shut it off.

"Relax," he said, "I'll handle this. By the way, did you like it?"

I looked over at him and my mouth worked, silently.

Finally I squeaked out, "Yes," in a small voice.

"Come on. Let's go get some lunch."

Victor stepped out first. He rushed around before I could get my door halfway open and swung it the rest of the way for me.

He offered his hand. I almost glanced at Father but I didn't dare, I could feel his eyes on me, burning my neck.

Victor did not pull back the offered hand. I didn't want to be rude.

Yes, that was it. I didn't want to be rude.

I took his hand. He pulled me to my feet and I stumbled a little, shocked by his strength. My hand landed on his chest. His very muscular chest. He smiled at me.

"Evelyn!" my father barked.

My hands shot to my sides, my eyes to the floor. I walked over without looking up, but I could *feel* Victor behind me, feel the strut in his step.

"Yeah, I just wanted to get a little air before I eat. Eve decided to tag along."

"Evelyn," Father corrected. "She is not to *tag along* with you again."

"She's a big girl. She can do what she likes."

Father took a warning step forward. I looked up, biting my lip. I wanted to sink into the ground and disappear.

Victor was smiling at him. Dismissing him. He waved his hand and turned to his mother.

"Let's go-"

Father's hands shot out and seized him buy the collar.

"Listen here, you little-"

I didn't know a person could move so fast.

Victor's hands shot up, between Father's arms, and he spread them wide, snapping my father's grip, sending him stumbling back. Victor's arms whirled, his feet spread, and he stood on bent, springy knees, his fists up.

"Victor!" his mother shouted.

He glanced at her, his expression wounded.

Victor's hands fell. For a moment. Then his right arm shot up and he jabbed his finger in my father's chest, hard enough to make him flinch.

"You want to play house with my mother, fine. You do not put your fucking hands on me in *my* house, am I clear? You wanna go, we'll go. Otherwise, keep your hands to yourself."

He looked at his mother, then glanced at me.

"I'm not hungry," he said, and brushed past my father to walk to the house.

Mrs. Amsel let out a long breath.

"He didn't mean any harm. They should get along."

"That thing," he looked at the car, "is dangerous. I won't have your son putting my daughter in danger, Karen."

"I wanted to go," I blurted out.

His eyes widened when he looked at me.

Mrs. Amsel sighed.

"Victor went to a private driving school, Martin. He knows what he's doing."

"Yes," Father said, his voice acid. "I'm sure he knows exactly what he's doing."

"Martin," Mrs. Amsel said, in a warning tone. "I'll talk to him. I'm sure he just wanted to meet her. They're going to be brother and sister, after all."

"*What?*"

She looked at me, blinking. "Hasn't your father told you, dear? We're getting married."

I swayed on my feet. I thought I might pass out. It was like all the blood just drained out of my head, like someone pulled the plug from a bathtub. The fury slid out of his face and he smiled warmly at me. I looked at his wife-to-be and my head started pounding.

"I'd like an aspirin, please," I said.

"Of course, sweetie. Come on, let's head inside."

"I think we should be going," Father said.

Karen gave him a curious look. "I thought you had a clear schedule."

"I'd rather give Victor some time to cool down. I'll talk to him tomorrow. Man to man."

She sighed. "Alright, if you insist. I'll call you tonight."

The way she smiled at him made her look very young.

For some reason, I felt a stab of fear for her.

Father took my hand and walked me to our car. With every step his grip got tighter, until my hand began to throb. I tugged at his grip a little, and he squeezed harder. I choked down a cry, knowing it would be worse if I made a scene.

"Get in the car, you little slut."

He let go. I rushed around and curled up in the front seat. He hadn't used that tone with me in years. I was good. I was *good*.

Father did not drive like Victor, at all. It was a long, slow drive back to the city, in total silence. Neither of us spoke until we arrived at home.

The first thing Father said was to Imelda.

"Get out," he snapped.

She gathered her things and was out of the house, dismissed for the day in five minutes.

"Wait for me upstairs," he said to me coldly, before walking into his office.

Every step was slow, like I was wearing shoes made of lead and walking in water. I closed the door but did not dare lock it, and sat on my bed, hands folded on my lap. I waited.

I waited.

Waited more.

Waited for an hour, without moving.

Finally the door swung open.

"You defied me," he said.

His words chilled me but it was the belt that caught my eyes. He had one in in his hands, in addition to the one looped through his trousers. I knew that belt. It was old and creaked when he folded it in half. A work belt, too wide for dress pant loops, made of old, careworn leather that was strange soft even if it was rigid and tough to bend.

"Stand up."

I stood up.

"Take off your dress."

It was like an icy fist punched me in the stomach, but I did it. I pulled it over my head, turned around and neatly folded it, laid the folded square of powder blue cloth at the foot of the bed and shivered, standing there in my underwear and bra.

"Lie down on the bed. Crossways."

I laid face down on the bed.

"You understand, I'm doing this for your own good."

The words struck me just before the belt did, on the backs of my thighs.

I didn't scream. I choked it down, but tears burned in my closed eyes, forced their way out and I sucked in a sobbing breath just in time for the second blow, and almost screamed. It came out as a gurgling cry. It *hurt*. Nothing hurt that much, not even when I was smaller and he would burn my arms with the old curling iron. I couldn't scream so I began sobbing and pleading instead, stop it please stop please stop, but the more I begged for mercy the faster the blows rained on my legs and then on my back, until I was curled up in a flinching ball, red lines of agony burning into my legs and back, and I thought I would die it hurt so much. I lost my voice pleading, lost to a rasping whisper. Only then did he finally stop.

"You will *not* speak to that boy ever again. If he touches you or speaks to you, you will come to me immediately. If I find out you have defied me in this, I will make you wish you'd never been *born*, do you understand?"

I swallowed, and choked out a yes.

"Clean yourself up, get dressed, and choose a take out menu for dinner. You will eat in here. I don't wish to suffer the sight of a defiant little cunt at dinner tonight."

I ended up doing the first two, but I never came to him to order food and he never sought me out. I knew better than to risk some petty slight angering him. He only called me *that* when he was truly enraged.

It was my fault. I brought it on myself. I should have known better. Boys were all bad, they were all poison. He told me over and over to stay away from them, or I'd end up like my mother. I should have known, but...

I liked him. He was nice. He wanted to show me his car. I liked it, too.

I sat at my vanity and scrubbed my face with a warm cloth. Showering after a whipping would be agony. I turned on the padded stool and looked at my back. I had to sit on the very edge; at least he didn't hit my backside with belt. My back was a network of angry red welts, some already turning black. I limped back to the bed and put on long cotton shirt, and laid face down on the bed. I pressed my face into the pillow and wept softly, wondering if I could hold my breath until I passed out and smother myself, just disappear. I needed a diversion but I didn't dare risk exposing the box of books under the back. If Father came back for whatever reason and caught me reading *Ravished by the Outlaw Duke*, I might be in for a second whipping.

It could be worse. At least I wasn't bleeding.

Somehow I managed to curl up in a ball and sleep. The next day I forced myself not to limp, not to scream in agony when he kissed my cheek and touched my back.

He was only looking out for me.

Six weeks later, the wedding was announced. We moved in to the Amsel estate beforehand.

I resolved never to be alone with Victor. I would peek outside my room and make sure he wasn't waiting before I emerged, I spent all my free time either locked behind my new door or with Father or his mother or with *someone*, even a member of the staff. I walked in fear, and the expansive halls of the house felt like a prison.

All except the library. There was a library and no one cared to stop me from exploring it. The room alone was as big as our house in the city, and full of more books than I'd ever seen in my life. They were organized by subject in shelves so tall I had to climb a ladder to reach the top shelves. Left to my own devices, I spent half of June exploring, learning where the books were. There was a whole section of paperback romance novels- they belonged to Victor's mother, and one at a time I snuck them out of the library and back to my room to read, stuck between stacks of books related to my business studies. There was an expansive library of business and financial texts in the library.

I found it all about as interesting as the paint on the walls, but things were expected of me. I would major in business and I would go to a top tier master's program. I would, end of story.

My bruises had faded into yellow marks the day I walked into the library and headed for the romances to slip back the book I'd borrowed.

"Oh my God, you read those?"

I nearly jumped out of my skin.

The room was all dark colors, earth tones, antique furniture and Persian carpets. Victor looked totally out of place on a padded leather chaise, a book propped on his lap. He sat so the light streamed through the windows behind him, motes of dust dancing in the rays. It made his hair glow, somehow.

I swallowed.

"Yes."

I hurriedly grabbed another book without looking and rushed for the door.

"Don't tell my father. Please."

"Tell him what?"

"Anything."

I pushed through the doors and scurried back to my room, praying. Don't let him see me. Don't let him see me. Don't let him see me. Only when I was back inside and the door locked did my heart stop pounding.

I was curled up in a side chair reading when a piece of lined notebook paper, folded in half, slipped up under my door.

Widow's Walk. Two AM, it read.

I opened the door and looked both ways, but there was no one there. I locked it again, looked at the clock.

Time for dinner.

Chapter Nine

Evelyn

I thought I was going to throw up.

The staircase to the widow's walk was in a closet. I'm sure it was just a door at some point, but it was converted to a closet, with the winding spiral staircase itself behind a false wall the swung open with a touch. It was dark inside, but clean. I was surprised. I expected a mouldering secret passage filled with cobwebs and critters. Three turns up, and there was another door that led out onto a long path that crossed the entire roof of the main house, lined with a tall wrought-iron railing tipped with wicked looking spikes. I touched one, and felt the sharpness of the edge, like a spear point. To my left was the big round cupola over the office, a room belonging to Victor's father that I never entered, having only seen it once when his mother gave me a tour. To the right, the woods and the road, further off.

Cicadas buzzed in the night. It was dark up here, but the moon and stars were out. More stars than I'd ever seen, so far away from the city.

Then, there was Victor. He leaned against the railing, arms folded over his chest.

I walked over, glancing either side, terrified someone would spot me. Victor was all in black. I wore a long, demure nightgown of heavy cotton. Would someone looking up think I was a ghost with bright blue eyes?

He looked over at me and stood up, towering over me.

"What's with you?"

I swallowed. "Nothing. I shouldn't be here. I'm sorry."

As I turned to leave, he grabbed my wrist.

Shock melted on his face when I looked back at him, trembling with fear. He let go immediately.

"I didn't mean to… wait!"

I stopped, gripped the horizontal part of the railing, and looked down. I could pitch myself off the roof. Maybe then I would be a ghost.

"What do you want?"

"I want to know why you're acting like this. You jump at shadows, you hide in your room all the time or follow my mom around. Something's not right."

"Everything is fine."

He studied me.

"You're lying," he said. "You lie a lot."

My lip trembled and I tucked it under my front teeth to stop it, and hugged myself. It was hot and muggy outside, but I was shivering.

"I have to go back to bed. I can't be seen…"

"Seen by who?"

"It doesn't matter."

"You're a big girl. My mother doesn't care what you do. So that leaves your father."

I didn't say anything, but he went on.

"He put his hands on me that day I took you for a ride. Does he ever put his hands on you?"

I tried not to, but I flinched with a shocked expression.

"I see," he said.

"No, he doesn't, he never. He's just protective of me, that's all."

"Mom said you were homeschooled."

"That's right."

"Why?"

"I... I couldn't go to regular school. I wouldn't fit in there."

"Why?"

"Because he said so."

Victor folded his big arms. The flexing of muscles stretched and distorted the feathers incised on his arms

"I like your tattoos," I blurted out.

"Thanks," he said, sounding slightly confused. "Does your father ever hit you?"

I tried to say *no, of course he doesn't*, but nothing would come out. My throat just went dry.

"I need to go. Please."

"There's nothing between you and the door."

I turned and rushed back, down the steps, and into the hallway without looking. Thankfully, I was alone. I almost went to my room, but headed for the kitchen instead. It was dark, but oddly well lit from the gleam on all the stainless steel. I poured myself a glass of water, choked it down in quick gulps, and went back to bed.

The wedding was scheduled for that Saturday. The next three days were the most tense of my life. I would be in the wedding party. Victor was giving his mother away, standing in for the father of the bride. A huge, far-flung extended family would be there. My mother's family would be there, people I hadn't seen in years.

Father came to me the day before. He sat beside me on my bed.

"Tomorrow," he said, "I expect you to socialize with the guests. Keep it to a minimum. You will also be expected to dance with Victor." His mouth twisted with distaste. "You understand why I am telling you this."

"Yes, sir."

"He's promiscuous. You matter too much to be a notch on his bedpost."

"Good. Get some sleep."

I woke the next day at five in the morning, and spent an hour pacing my bedroom. The wedding was at ten, not in the city but a little town nearby. The house was full of guests, mostly Victor's extended family. By the time I bathed and dressed and put my hair in a simple braid, Karen was already gone to get ready away from the house. Victor went with her. Father's best man was a friend from the firm. My dress was demure and not particularly flattering but he kept eyeing me, as did another of Father's guests, a Russian man that introduced himself as Vitali and held my gloved hand too long. I rode in another car, with one of Mrs. Amsel's relatives.

The church was old, and packed, every seat taken. I sat up front near the altar. Victor walked his mother down the aisle, a forced smile on his face, heat in his eyes when he looked at my father, waiting in a morning coat with swallow tails. He hated this, I realized. He didn't want my father marrying his mother. He didn't want any of this. He glanced at me as he stepped away from my mother. The priest talked, but it was all buzzing to me. I rose when everyone else did, sat when they did, watched my father slip a ring on his mother's finger and watched him kiss her, passionately. I clapped when the others clapped, but my hands when still when I saw Victor standing stock still during the applause. A little

143

girl I didn't know carried his mother's train and another sprinkled flowers. Rice was thrown, and Victor stiffly took my arm and led me to the limousine for the wedding party.

He didn't say a word to me on the drive to the reception. He offered me his arm again without looking at my father as we went into the fire hall. I glanced at Father and he gave me a tiny nod, and I stiffly took Victor's arm and walked to the table with him. It took twenty minutes for the guests to file in.

Victor sat next to his mother. I sat next to Father. Three courses were served, after the toast. I didn't hear any of it. The world buzzed in my ears, like the insistent rushing of a stream. I just wanted to go home. I sat there pawing the folds of my skirts and barely touched my food.

Soon I would be free, I realized. I would be going to college, living on campus.

Except I'd never be free. Father would always know if I did something I shouldn't. If I was bad.

People started standing. I missed the announcement. It was time for the cake, and the dancing.

Oh, and the bouquet.

Before I realized it I was lined up with twenty other unmarried girls, all strangers. I wanted to run and hide. Victor's mother turned around, faced away from all of us. She pitched the bouquet back over her head. I watched it sail through the air towards us and held my ground as the other girls moved forward. I held my hands out limply, pretending that I wanted to catch it. Father would be furious if it came at me and I let it hit the floor. He didn't believe in inane superstitions like bad luck from dropping some flowers. I was sure it was coming right at me, until another girl snatched it from the air in front of me. I let out a palpable sigh of relief and shuffled away as soon as I could, while people surrounded and cheered the girl.

Then the single men started gathering around. I blinked a few times. What was that about? Victor stood in front, scowling.

His mother turned, hiked up her voluminous cream skirts, and stuck out her stocking-clad leg. My father smiled at her, his expression going blank as he knelt. He thought no one saw. No one did, but me. He slid her garter down her leg, careful not to disturb their stocking, and put on a false smile as he stood up, twirled it around his finger, and threw it.

Victor shoved another unmarried man out of the way and plucked it from the air.

Oh. Oh God.

He looked over at me and beckoned me forward. The girl with the bouquet turned red and scowled. Everyone was staring.

"Come on, Eve," Victor said, loudly.

I looked at my father, but Karen grinned at me.

"What are you waiting for?"

Somebody whistled behind me. Catcalls started. I shuffled forward and stood stiff as a board, unsure what I was supposed to do. Finally I realized he was supposed to put it on my leg.

Which meant I had to hike up my skirts. I did, and stuck out my leg. Victor knelt in front of me, and gently cupped my foot in his hand. He slipped off my shoe, and pulled the elastic band up over my calf, then up my thigh. I shivered as his fingers brushed the skin of my leg, and bit my lip.

It felt… good. He held my calf lightly in his hand and put my shoe back on, and I lowered my foot to the floor. As I put my foot down he stood up, rising inches away from me, his face filling my vision as I stood to my full height.

Karen was grinning. Father's face was a stony mask, a false smile stretched over absolute, incandescent fury.

The disk jockey started talking. Victor took my arm and walked me, briskly, away from the open floor. It was time for the first dance of the bride and groom. Karen was absolutely overjoyed, smiling so much it had to hurt. She put her head on Father's chest as they danced, and he looked genuinely happy.

Except for his eyes. His eyes never changed.

The best man danced with the maid of honor, a girl I didn't know, one of Karen's people. I tried to slink into the crowd.

Victor took my wrist and pulled me out onto the dance floor.

"I've never danced before," I blurted out.

"Me either, not like this. It's not hard. We just stand close together and walk around. No big deal."

I nodded. It was no big deal, until he put his hand on the small of my back, and clasped my hand in his. My heart started pounding and my throat went dry. There was a distance between us, maybe six inches between our stomachs, but it felt like we were touching anyway. I stared at his throat and didn't look at anyone, aimlessly moving in a circle, shuffling my feet. He squeezed my hand.

"Does he hurt you?" Victor murmured.

"Who?"

"Your father."

I shook my head and looked away from him.

"Time for the cake."

He let go of my hand, and his palm fell away from my waist. He stood next to me, arms folded, as our parents fed each other sickly sweet wedding cake. I ended up with a paper plate in my hand, picking at a slice. The icing was too cloying sweet and I wanted to spit it out.

"This cake sucks," Victor grumbled.

I couldn't help it. I started laughing.

There were a few looks, but no one paid me much mind. They probably thought I was laughing from happiness at the wonderful wedding. I dumped my cake on a random table and looked for a place I could hide. I never liked crowds and it felt like there was an itchy wool blanket on my shoulders, weighing me down. I tugged on my skirts and wove my way through the crowd, and ended up in front of the fire hall. I breathed in warm, humid evening air. Music thudded through the brick walls as I sat down on a narrow ledge running through the windows and plucked at loose strands of my hair. A shadow fell across my feet.

I looked up and Victor pushed a glass of red liquid at me. There was a little umbrella in it.

"I can't drink."

"Me either. Not here, anyway. It's a Shirley Temple."

I took it and sipped it through the little straw. It was too sweet, but it was cold and liquid. Victor had one, too. He seemed amused by the umbrella. After he finished the drink he took it out and was playing with it, popping it up and down.

"These aren't supposed to have umbrellas. Want another one?

"I shouldn't be talking to you."

"Why?"

I was trying to think of an answer when I heard a piercing voice.

"Victor!"

I looked over to see a girl our age storm outside. Her dress made me blush. I was honestly wondering how it stayed up. It had no back or sleeves, just cups for her rather large breasts. She walked over and planted her fists on her hips, a long leg visible through a high slit in the side of her skirt.

"Uh," he said.

"Amber."

"Right. Hi, Amber."

"What are you doing out here?" she demanded.

"Getting some air. I brought Eve something to drink."

I looked at her but she ignored me. Instead she tugged his arm.

"Come inside. What was that about, giving *her* the garter?"

He shook loose of her grip. She scowled at him.

"What are you doing here?" he said.

"You invited me," she said, folding her arms under her impressive bust.

"I did?"

"*Yes,*" she growled.

I stood up. Neither of them noticed me. I took my cup and Victor's, and walked back inside. I found a trash can, tossed the little plastic cups and looked at the clock. When would this be over? I just wanted to be alone.

The reception had moved onto the dance floor, so I walked back into the dining room and sat down at my seat. It wasn't five minutes before Victor slunk in and sat down next to me. In my father's seat, I noticed.

"What do you want?"

"You look upset."

"Shouldn't you be occupied with Amber?"

151

"Don't worry about her. She kinda crashed the wedding."

"I see."

I folded my hands primly in my lap. Maybe if I just sat there he'd leave.

"I'm sorry if I got you in trouble."

"About what?"

"The car. The day we met. I wouldn't have done that if I knew your father would flip out."

"You wouldn't?"

"Maybe I would have. Mom was worried about you. She said you were really upset. Did I piss you off?"

I look over at him, then away, and sigh. "No. Not me."

"I know he was upset, but I *do* know what I'm doing. You want some more cake? Something to eat? A drink?"

"Why?"

He shrugged. "Look, I'll be honest. I don't know most of these people. The ones I do know I hate. Three of my ex-girlfriends showed up, invited by my mother. Your father tried to kill me with his eye lasers when I gave you the garter."

"I don't think that was appropriate," I said. "Our parents are married now. We can't…"

"What?" he said, smirking.

"Nothing."

"We can't nothing? That's a double negative."

Flustered, I rubbed at my temples.

"I know, it's shocking. I read a book."

"I can't talk to you," I blurted out.

"Why? Did somebody threaten you? Your dad?"

"Why do you keep asking me that?"

"Why'd you come up to the widows walk? You *want* to tell me, you just *won't*. Look, this guy just married my mom. If he's trouble I need to know."

I look around the empty dining room. The crowd in the dance hall starts to blur as my eyes burn.

"He disciplines me. That's all. I broke a rule. I needed punishment."

Victor looked at me intently.

"Punished you how?" he said, softly.

I covered my mouth with my hand and stifled a sob.

"I can't. Don't make me tell you. I *can't*."

"I don't want to make you do anything."

I sat there and sniffed quietly until he found a clean napkin and handed it to me. I snatched it and rubbed at my eyes and nose. It only made my nose raw.

"You moved into my house. My roof. Your father married my mother but the house is *mine*."

"Are you mad at her? For getting married again?"

He sighs. "Yes, but don't tell her that. It's not… she's been alone for over six years. She doesn't fit into my dad's social circles. She was a waitress before they married. She's completely alone. Your father spent a lot of time with her. They got to know each other, started seeing each other, I was fine with it. I think he had me fooled."

"Fooled?"

"You don't have to tell me what he does to you. It's probably better if you don't. He does hurt you though, doesn't he? You're scared shitless of him."

I started wringing the napkin in my hands. "He spanked me when I was younger. That's all."

"When you were younger," Victor said, carefully.

"A-after the car ride," I choked out.

"With his hand?"

"No. He uses a belt."

His hand clenched into a fist, his knuckles bleeding of color as he crushed the tablecloth in his hand. "Not anymore. He puts a hand on you again, or a belt or anything else, you come to me, understand?"

I nodded, not knowing what to say.

"I wish you'd told me before. I would have put a stop to this."

"He'd kill me," I blurted out.

Victor looked up. "What?"

"I didn't mean it. You know how people say 'he'd kill me," I added quickly.

"No. You meant it."

I swallowed.

"I'm thirsty. Will you get me something to drink?"

"Yeah."

He came back from the bar with another sweet, alcohol-free cocktail. I drank it quickly. I thought he brought the second one for himself, but he gave that one to me, too.

"You were home schooled," he said.

"Yes."

"You weren't around any other kids? Ever?"

"No. I wasn't allowed."

He scratched his neck. "Jesus. You're supposed to start college this fall?"

"Yes."

"I want you to call me if you get in any kind of trouble."

"Why?"

He shrugged. "I guess I'm your big brother now."

I scowled at him.

He touched the back of my neck lightly with his fingers. It turned into a caress.

"I wish we weren't."

I stood up. "I should go back to the dance floor. I'll be missed."

"Wouldn't want that, would we? You go, I'll wait a bit. Wouldn't want Daddy Dearest to think we were making out in the bathroom."

I was a mess, but it was dark out there. People were milling around more than dancing. I thought it would be over soon. I hoped so.

Chapter Ten

Evelyn

Moving day.

I didn't take all my things. I packed two large suitcases, two small ones, a bag of toiletries and few odds and ends, like bed linens for a twin mattress. Karen went with us. Victor did not. The topic was never raised and I never asked what he was doing at the time. The Firebird was gone from the garage on the day I moved. The servants carried my things out to the car. Father purchased a new one not long after the wedding, a BMW sedan. I rode in the back seat, while Karen sat next to Father. I didn't want to sit next to him. I kept my face a mask, but the whole world felt itchy. I was giddy and terrified at the same time. I was going to be free. I was going to get away from him. I had no plans to do anything radically different, but it would be a relief not to watch every word I spoke, every gesture, every movement for fear he'd see some wrong in it and punish me. He didn't even go through my bags, so my books were coming with me. Karen even let me take a few from the library.

So far, this was my second trip to the college. There was a tour in July. I went, with Father, and saw the dorm where I would be living, but I hadn't been assigned a room yet. I was on the second floor, in an all-girls dormitory. When we arrived I had to check in first. Father blessedly let me handle that, walking around a row of tables in a conference room. It was a small institution- a single large X-shaped complex of four halls and a College Center in the middle, four dormitory buildings and one detached hall of classrooms. Registration took place in the main building, near a little store that sold snacks. I was terrified the entire time, staring at my feet. I'd never been with so many people my own age. We arrived early. Check-in began at eight in the morning and I walked in at seven fifty-three. I had my official identification card by eight thirty. Then we walked to the dormitory, to get my key and start moving in.

"This is a lovely campus," Karen said. "Nice town, too. I think you'll have a wonderful time here, Eve."

I was growing closer to my stepmother than I anticipated. She spent most of her day *doing things*, in a way I never really experienced before. She had a dozen hobbies, all sorts of interests, and she read and had a sharp mind. I understood why Victor's father married her.

I thought I was starting to understand why my father married her, too. It unnerved me. He'd bought a whole new wardrobe, new watches, the new car. I wasn't stupid. I knew he was spending her money. I didn't have an idea about their finances. My understanding was that Victor was the heir to the family fortune, but I didn't ask about it. I wasn't interested. I just wanted out.

My key was in a small envelope in a box with my name on it. The Resident Director gave me papers to sign. I promised to attend a Freshman Mixer, whatever that would turn out to be.

The room was small, barely eight feet wide, but almost fifteen feet long. A bunk bed sat in the corner, opposite from that two desks sitting next to each other, and two armoires- there was no closet built into the wall. We all carried my things in. It took all of ten minutes.

Father put his hand on my shoulder and I flinched.

"Alright, Eve. We're going to go now, so you can get settled in."

Karen looked at me.

"Can I have a minute alone with her?"

Father nodded, and stepped outside. I heard his shoes on the hallway floor.

Karen threw her arms around me.

"You call me if you need anything, or you just want to talk. Alright, hon?"

"Yes, Karen," I said.

My chest tightened and my eyes burned. I was supposed to be happy? Why was I starting to cry?

"This is going to be a big shock for you. I mean it. Call me for help if you need it," she reached into her purse and handed me a slip of paper. "Or call Victor. He's closer."

I took the paper.

"He likes you."

My eyes snapped up to meet hers.

"My son has always been difficult," she sighed, lowering her voice. "He has quite a reputation, and with good reason. When he grew older, without his father around, I had a lot of trouble controlling him. There were fights. There were a lot of girls. I never saw him look at any of them the way he looks at you."

"We can't, he's…"

"He's my son. You're not my daughter."

I wilted, looking at the floor.

She rested her hand on my shoulder and squeezed. "I didn't mean it that way. I wish you were."

Tell her, I screamed at myself. *He's a monster, you married a monster. He wants something from you, or else he'd never touch you. He hits me, he hurt me.* Say something!

I didn't. She hugged me again and I hugged her back, no matter how awkward I felt. I wondered what it would be like to have my own mother here, holding me. Then I walked out of the building with her, and waved goodbye as they drove off.

When I got back to the room there was a stranger in it. She startled me.

For a brief moment, I thought she was a man. It was the height. She was six feet tall, even in flat tennis shoes, and simply towered over me, but there was nothing else manly about her. Her clothes were as baggy and unflattering as mine, and she didn't appear to be wearing any makeup, but she was pretty anyway, in a natural way. The most striking thing about her was her hair, wound in a long braid that hung almost to her waist, a rich auburn that shone like beaten copper when the sun hit it. She looked as started as I was, and for a moment she just stood there and stared at me. Then she thrust out her hand and took it.

"Hi. I'm Jennifer."

We'd emailed, but there wasn't much to say. She moved gracefully around the room, left and came back with a suitcase.

"Don't you have anyone to help you?"

She shook her head.

"I will," I said.

She had a car, a battered little Toyota. It was stuffed with suitcases and boxes and bags, like she'd packed all her worldly goods into the back and the seats. It took us an hour to unload it all. I started moving my things to the top bunk when we finished, and she stopped me.

"You got here first."

"That's not really fair."

She shrugged. "Maybe we could flip for it?"

"Well, you're bigger, you should be on the bottom."

She blinked a few times. Her lip trembled.

"I don't mean bigger like fat," I said, quickly. "You're taller than me, that's all."

This was getting off to a first class start.

"I'll take the top," she insisted.

After she made up her bed, I was shocked by how easily she got up there, with a fluid grace I wasn't expecting from someone of her height.

"Are you going to that mixer thing?" she asked, leaning over the side.

I was still making up my bed. I had to put hospital corners on my sheets. "Of course. I signed a paper promising I would."

"I don't think they really care," she said.

"Are you going?"

"I don't want to," she shrugged, and leaned back onto her bed. "I hate parties."

"I've never been to a party."

She let out a long sigh. "Consider yourself fortunate," she said.

That was a rather odd thing to say, but I didn't want to pry.

I really, truly was not planning to go, but I signed a form. They would know if I didn't. It was scheduled for six o'clock, in daylight, so there were no worries there. Around five thirty I got up from reading on my bed.

"I'm going to go to the thing," I said.

"It's across the street. You'll be very early."

I shrugged. "On time is late."

She rolled over and looked at me. She had gray eyes too, I noticed.

"You haven't *ever* been to a party, have you?"

I shook my head. "You weren't allowed to go?"

"Never invited."

"Oh."

"There was no one *to* invite me. I was home schooled. Tutors."

I shifted uncomfortably on my feet and rubbed my arms. Jennifer sat up, and slid to the floor with the same languid grace with which she'd climbed up. She spun her desk chair around and sat on it facing backwards, leaning on the back.

"We're supposed to talk," she said.

I sat down on the bed.

"What should we talk about?"

"Thank you for helping me carry my things. I appreciate it."

"You have a lot of stuff."

She shrugged. "It's everything I own. I'm not going back. I already signed the papers to stay here over the winter break. I'm going to be in the room a lot. I hope you don't mind."

"Okay."

"Um," she said, her face turning red. "I don't like undressing around people. Have you been to the showers?"

"Yes, it's not like a movie. There's stalls with curtains."

She shuddered. "I'll make do. I might ask you to step out of the room now and then."

"I can do that." I shrugged.

"I'll be in here a lot. I don't go out much. I don't have a boyfriend or anything."

"Neither do I."

"Oh." She sounded surprised.

"Um," I said, searching for something else to talk about. I would be leaving soon if I wanted to be on time. "What are you majoring?"

"English. I want to teach. You?"

"Business," I sighed.

"You don't sound excited about it."

"I'm not. I should be going now. Are you coming?"

"No," she said, firmly. "I don't do parties. Oh, that's the other thing. No parties in our room, please. No drinking."

"I'm not old enough to drink, and I don't know anybody."

She nodded, and seemed reassured. "Thank you.

True to her word, Jennifer climbed up on her bunk and remained in the room. Walking through that door was like passing through a brick wall. I had to force myself to take every step. I expected there to be a stream of students on the sidewalk.

There were a few, but no one seemed to be in any hurry to get to "the mixer". There was some sort of a stage set up on the lawn in front of the college center and people appeared to be setting up a sound system. When they tested it with a burst of music, the speakers whined and popped. I felt a vibration through my feet. It turned into a sound, a throaty basso rumble that echoed off the brick buildings. As I turned to see where it was coming from, I let out a slow breath. Victor's Pontiac came rumbling down the street. He pulled up behind me and motioned me over.

Against my better judgement, I walked over to the car. I looked around, hoping no one would see me talking to him.

"Hey" he almost shouted, his voice raised over the exhaust. "Need a ride?"

"I have to go to the freshman mixer."

He laughed. "Are you serious? No, you don't. Hop in. You eat dinner yet?"

"No, I thought there would be food at the mixer."

"There's food at McDonalds. Come on."

I looked back over to the lawn and chewed my lip.

"You're thinking about it. That means I've already won. I promise no one will even know if you're there or not."

"I can't, Victor. I'm not supposed to even talk to you."

He leaned out the window a little. "Come on."

"Are you going to speed?"

"No way. I promise to obey all traffic controls and speed limits." He raised his hand in an I-swear gesture.

I took a deep breath, then walked around and got in the car. True to his word, Victor rumbled gradually down the block, and took the turn slowly.

It was a bit quieter inside the car.

"What are you even doing here?"

"What? Oh, right, I'm a student here."

"*You?*"

"I transferred."

"What?"

He fished in his pocket and pulled out a student identification card just like mine, with his smiling face on it. I looked over at him and tugged on my seat belt. I noticed he wasn't bothering to wear his.

"You should eat. You eat anything today?"

I shook my head.

"Okay, burger time, then."

I tugged at my jeans, trying to gather the material in my hands. I ended up pitching forward with my arms folded over my chest.

He didn't ask me any questions. I watched out the window as he drove. At the restaurant, Victor opened my door for me and took my hand to pull me to my feet. He made a show of it, flexing his muscles. I really didn't need his help. He walked close beside me, opened the doors for me. I walked up to the counter with him.

I had no idea what to get. I'd never eaten at one of these before.

"Um," I said. "I don't know what to…"

Victor stepped up to the counter. "Two double quarter pounders with cheese, a quarter pounder with cheese, a large french fries, a strawberry milkshake," he glanced at me, "and two large sodas."

He paid, too, and carried the tray. I sat down at the table he chose and gingerly unwrapped my cheeseburger, feeling the grease on my fingers. I lifted the bun-lid and frowned at the gunk on top, took a napkin and swept it off.

"I didn't know you like them plain. Sorry."

"I've never had one." I pointed at the pile of lettuce and tomato. "I just don't want that."

"Works for me," he said, and did the same thing to his. He ate one of his sandwiches so fast it was almost unnerving to watch. I'd filled my cup with orange soda. I like oranges. It was so *sweet*.

He put the milk shake up in front of me. "This is for you."

"It is?"

He gave me a look.

I shrugged and took a pull on the straw. It was too sweet, too.

The burger was better than I thought it would be. I like having a little of the... stuff on it. The milk shake wasn't bad, either.

"You've seriously never eaten here before?"

"I've never had occasion to."

"I mean at any of the chain stores."

"Victor," I said.

"Vic," he corrected.

"Vic. What do you want from me?"

He gave me an enigmatic smile and a shrug. "You really don't know, do you?"

Vic reached over and set his hand on mine.

I tensed.

"Oh. *Oh.*"

"You're not good with signals, are you?"

I shook my head.

He sighed.

My face reddened. I could feel it. He smiled, not so much for me as at me, his eyes darting all over my face and neck. I pulled my hand back and folded both together in my lap.

"I can't. I'm your sister."

He snorted. "Yeah, for like a month and a half."

"I already heard people commenting about us dancing at the wedding. Then there was the garter thing."

He leaned on his hand. "Fuck them."

I flinched.

"Eve, do you like me? I think you like me. I like you."

"I think I do. I don't... I don't know. I don't know what to do," my voice cracked. "I don't know how to talk to anybody or what to do or what to say or..." I trailed off. "I can't. I can't do it. If Father finds out..."

"If he puts his hands on you I'll break his legs."

I jerked back and looked at him. "He's my father."

"Yeah. He is. My father never hit me. He never hit my mom either. He could have, if he wanted. He was a big guy. He taught me a lot."

"My father taught me a lot," I said.

"I can see that. My father taught me a man must have a code."

"A code?"

"Yeah."

I swallowed, took a big gulp of milkshake and dabbed at my lips with a napkin.

"I just want you to give me a chance. I'm not asking you to marry me. I'm not going to lock you in a tower and 'ravish' you like in one of those books you read."

My mouth fell open.

"My mom told me."

Something about that was funny enough for me to start laughing.

"People have told me things about you."

"Such as?"

I started wringing my fingers.

"You sleep with lots of girls. You don't really care about me, I'd just be another…" what was it? "Notch on your bedpost."

"That's a fun trick."

I blinked. "What?"

"You talk, and your father's voice comes out."

My mouth worked silently. I looked at him, without looking away, the way he was looking at me. Just *looking* at someone had never made feel this way before.

"What do I do? I mean, if I want to be your girlfriend. Um."

I sounded like an idiot. I knew it even then.

"You don't do anything. We hang out. Do stuff together."

"Like what?"

"I can think of a few things."

Chapter Eleven

Evelyn

"He can't be in here," Jennifer said coldly, scowling at me from her top bunk.

"He's not staying. Besides, we can have guests until ten o'clock."

"Nice to meet you, too," Victor smirked at her. "I guess this means I'm dropping you off."

"Yes."

"Classes don't start until Monday. We should go out tomorrow."

"Alright."

Victor stood there, a wry smirk on his face. I wasn't sure what I was supposed to do, so I shifted from one foot to the other and worked my fingers, hoping he would give me some signal. His eyebrow rose and his smile widened a little, and then he put his hands on my shoulders, leaned down, and pressed his lips to mine.

I didn't know what to *do*. Did I just stand there. I pushed back a little, turned my head. It was pleasurable when I felt his lips move against mine. It felt good. His lips tugged on my bottom lip as he pulled away, and my chest fluttered. I felt strangely excited, like I wanted to start bouncing on my heels. He tucked a loose strand of hair behind my ear and his fingers traced down the side of my neck and made me shiver. It was like a tickle, but different. I smiled dully.

It was my first kiss.

"I'll be around," he said, and squeezed my arm.

"Nice to meet you," he nodded at Jennifer.

Vic strode out of the room. I rushed over and locked the door, went back to my new desk and sat in the old chair in a daze.

"He's trouble," Jennifer said in a cold voice, and rolled over to face the wall.

I gave her back a withering look, but she didn't seem to notice. She ignored me completely as she tossed and turned, sat up, dug a book out of her bags and climbed back up with a little reading lamp.

"I get up early," she said, seemingly to no one in particular.

"So do I. Lights out?"

"If you wouldn't mind."

I turned off the overhead light and climbed into bed. Her reading lamp lit the room softly for maybe an hour, then clicked off. I curled up tried to sleep, but sleep wouldn't come. All I could think about was the way he touched me. It was just my arms, but no one ever really *touched* me. Then there was the kiss. I thought it was awkward, but I liked it. I wondered what it would be like to kiss the way they did in movies, open mouthed, writhing around, bodies pressed together in passionate heat. I pressed my legs together, too. I felt itchy, and hot even though the air conditioning made me shiver. I tucked up under my blanket and tried again to sleep, tried to clear my head and think about nothing. I should have fallen asleep easily. I was tired, I'd been awake all day, in the car and carrying things and unpacking. I had a full stomach.

Sleep stalked me for hours but never pounced. When I finally dozed off it must have been in the wee hours of the morning, and it was a fitful sleep. When my roommate made the slightest move or sound, I snapped awake. I'd never shared a room with a person before, and every movement made me think *intruder*.

I had a dream.

Everything was huge, like some torturous funhouse. Chairs were too high to climb, the carpet monstrously huge, scraping my tiny feet as I walked. I was in a strange place, a huge empty place. Sheets covered all the furnishings like ghosts, and there were light squares on the walls, specters of lost paintings. Boxes everywhere, a maze of them. There was something behind me, following me, stalking, moving closer. I looked over my shoulder and saw him. My father, gigantic and stooped, his head scraping the ceiling. His eyes burned with blue flames, like a gas stove, charred the skin around his too-big eye sockets. I screamed and ran and he chased after me on back-jointed legs, snapping a belt in his huge bony hands. The belt was made of strange pale leather, as wide as my hands and studded with gleaming metal points, wickedly sharp. I ran and ran and ran and called a name without remembering it.

All at once the world began shifting around me, jerking wildly, and I fell. In a dark corner I saw the figure of a woman, hunched and weeping, but she had no face, only a blank void where eyes and nose and mouth should be. She reached a hand for me in mute appeal, but her fingers were broken. The shaking grew worse, the world tumbling and turning around me, and I forgot I was being chased and he was *there*.

You've been difficult, you little slut. Take off your dress and wake up.

Wake up.

"Wake up," Jennifer snapped at me, not gently but not angrily, either.

My head came up from the pillow. I was covered head to toe in cold, acid sweat. The light outside was still bruised from dawn, and cut lines on the tile floor through the blinds. Jennifer quickly drew her hand back from my shoulder as I curled up in a ball, twisted up in my blankets, and lay there panting.

She crouched next to the bed.

"You started shouting in your sleep. I don't understand what you were saying."

"Oh. Sorry. I had a bad dream."

She gave me a cryptic nod. "Can you stay in the bed for a second?"

I nodded, and she gracefully slipped back up into the top bunk. I heard her shift around, the bed jerked, and she came down in a crouch, dressed in sweatclothes, and slipped on a pair of running shoes.

No one I've ever met exercised as much as she did. She was either studying, sleeping, or running or, later, riding a bicycle. She seemed to live on granola bars and cold oatmeal.

While Jennifer was out running, I went to the showers for the first time. It made me nervous, but there was plenty of privacy, a big curtain for each stall and room to change in front of the shower itself.

After that I didn't know what to do with myself, so I took my schedule and went to the book store. I came back with two armloads of plastic bags, the handles cutting into my fingers, and neatly stacked the books on the little shelf on my desk. For the next hour or so, I started reading a microeconomics textbook, tapping my foot on the tiles. There was a tap at my window, a soft sound on the glass, then another, and another. I looked over and saw Victor peering through the glass at me, grinning.

My room was on the second floor.

I threw up the sash.

"What are you doing?"

"Let me in."

I fumbled with the screen, lifted it up. The windows were very large. I jumped out of the way as Victor clambered inside. He was barefoot, his shoes hanging from his belt, tied by their laces. He wiped sweat off his forehead with his hand, then scooped me up in his arms. He literally lifted me off the floor as he pulled me against him, and kissed me. This time I touched him back, putting my hands on his sides, just above his hips. The muscles bunched and tightened under his skin as he moved. The kiss was like a mouthful of warm honey, and left me breathless and shaking. He put his arms around me.

"What are you up to?"

"Reading," I said, glancing at the book.

"What is that?"

"*Principles of Microeconomics, Third Edition.*"

"You're reading a *textbook?*"

"What?"

He grinned at me. "I didn't think you were that boring."

"I'm not boring." I sighed. "The book is boring."

"You'll have time to read that later. Come with me."

"Where?"

"Anywhere but here."

Jennifer picked that moment to come back. She walked in, gathered up her robe and toiletry bag, and left, all while scowling at Victor.

"I think she's starting to like me."

"I don't think she likes you at all."

He sighed. "One day you will understand this. We earth humans call it 'humor'."

"Oh. You were being sarcastic."

"Yeah. She has a key, right? Come on."

I locked up and followed him outside. He parked in the overflow, tucking the Firebird into a corner space so the car in the next spot over was far enough away to swing the wide door open. As always, he opened mine first before getting in himself. I unlocked his door for him.

"So where are we going?"

"You have anything in mind?"

"Not really," I said. "I don't know what to do if I'm not studying."

"You know, they have a drive-in down here."

"A drive-in theater? It's what, ten in the morning? It won't be dark for hours."

"Hours and hours," said Victor. "We'll just have to find something to do until then. I have an idea. Have you ever been to the beach?"

"No."

"Let's go. It's only about an hour drive. If you obey all traffic control devices and posted speed limits."

The way he said it strongly implied he didn't plan on it.

"Okay."

I've never seen any of this before. I stared out the windows as he drove. The whole place was so *flat*. I could see for miles and miles, the distance obscured only by trees here and there, or buildings. It wasn't like home, where the rode rose and fell. I expected the ocean to be something like the river. Living in Philadelphia, my idea of the coastline was the Delaware river. A few times I glanced over at the instrument cluster, and felt my stomach drop when I realized we were topping ninety miles an hour. Except for a few gentle curves, the road was mostly straight. Victor slowed dramatically when a sign appeared warning of the end of the expressway, and the traffic grew heavier. He turned off past a car dealership, and the car rumbled over an iron bridge over a narrow canal.

"You've seriously never been here?"

I shook my head.

"No trips to Jersey, either? No Cape May, no Atlantic City?"

"No."

"Wow. I came down here with Mom all the time. She liked to shop at the outlets. When Dad was alive we came here every weekend in the summer."

There it was.

The land just… ended. Victor pulled into a slanted parking space and I stepped out of the car. The air smelled salty and was strangely cool when the breeze picked up, even if the sun was hot on my skin. Victor slipped a pocket full of quarters into the parking meter and came to my side.

"You're going to burn up," he said, taking my arm. "Come on."

The air conditioning was blasting in the shop. Gooseflesh rose on my arms as Victor led me through the store. He grabbed a floppy straw hat off a rack, a big pair of sunglasses, and a bottle of sun screen. Outside, I put on the hat and glasses. It was a relief not to have to squint. Victor kept the sunscreen. He squirted a generous helping on his hand and seized my arm, rubbing it into my skin. I tried to shake loose, but he was insistent. He did my other arm, and then crouched and smeared it on my legs. I yelped as his hand came up between my thighs. Victor grinned and dabbed a spot of it on the tip of my nose. I scowled at him but he grinned and smeared the stuff on his own arms, tossed the bottle, still half full, into a trash can and pulled me to him by the waist. I grabbed my hat on the brim to keep him from knocking it off.

My anger melted away when his lips met mine.

People were *seeing* us. I felt naked, and for some reason that made me press against him, and he put his arms around my waist.

He took my hand and walked me down the sidewalk to see the ocean for the first time.

I stopped at the edge of the boardwalk and just stared, gaping like a fool. It was *huge*. I'd never seen anything so big. The wind was strong, and the waves were surging, whitecaps forming as the water rolled in and fell back, rolled in and fell back with a tremendous roar that came from everywhere at once. It was so *blue*. I walked across the boards and leaned on the railing.

"Too bad you don't have a bathing suit. We could go for a swim."

"In *that?*"

"What, are you scared?"

"Yes."

I was terrified of drowning. I had no idea how to swim, either. I'd never even been in a pool. The idea of diving into that deep dark water rooted me to the spot, terrified.

Victor's arms slid around me from behind.

"I wouldn't let anything happen to you."

"I can't swim."

"We'll have to fix that, sometime."

"What about sharks?"

"I don't think anybody has ever been attacked here."

186

"Maybe another day," I said, my voice trailing off.

"What do you think?"

"It's beautiful," I said.

"Yeah, Victor leaned on the rail. He wasn't looking at the ocean at all. "Beautiful. I guess you've never been to Funland."

"Fun…land?"

"Yeah, come on."

He took my hand and pulled me along with him. The sea breeze whipped around my legs and chilled me, even as the sun beat down, so I was shivering and sweating at the same time. The light was hot on my skin, and Victor's hand was warm. We walked past a dozen little shops, full of candy and toys and food. Ahead was this Funland place he mentioned, a small amusement park that covered a whole block. We walked past some carnival games. Blinking lights and chimes and music assaulted my ears. It was more than I could take. I almost clung to Victor, clasping his hand in mine. He bought a ream of little tickets at a booth, after we stood in line for a good five minutes.

"They'll close next weekend," he said.

"Forever?"

"Nah, for the season. It gets too cold, I guess. Come on. You need to try the frogs."

I wasn't sure what 'the frogs' meant until he led me over to a broad artificial pond. Fake lily pads floated around in circles, carrying cups shaped like flowers. A dollar bought three battered rubber frogs. The object of the game was to use a little catapult to hurl the frogs into the cups. It worked by bashing it with a hammer, which he handed to me. I did my best to line up the catapult with the moving cup and bashed it with the hammer.

My frog flew wildly and fell in the water with a heavy splash. That meant I lost.

"Try again."

My second try went no better than the first.

Victor slipped behind me. His arms came up around mine and he clasped his hands around mine as my back pressed to his chest. I wasn't thinking about the frogs. He lifted my hands and brought the hammer down. The frog went flying, too high I thought, and came down with a solid thump on the edge of one of the cups. It hung there for a moment and I thought it would slide into the water, until it rolled in. The attendant brought over a small stuffed rabbit and handed it to me.

"Let's do some rides," said Victor, taking my hand.

"Which one?"

He pointed at the far end of the little park. There was a huge viking longboat with a dragon head on either end, swinging back and forth until it went from horizontal to just past vertical.

"I am not riding that," I declared.

"Oh, come on. Look at all the people doing it. We'll be fine."

Somehow, he ended up pulling me into the line with him. My heart pounded harder the closer we came to getting on. I almost ducked into the exit line when he handed over the tickets for our spots on the ride, but he gave my hand a squeeze and pulled me along with him.

"It's not as bad if we sit at the end," he said.

Like a fool, I believed him.

A cross bar tightened over my legs, and I clung to Victor for dear life, hugging his arm and clutching my rabbit. He pulled my hat off and held it in his other hand, and the boat started to swing. It was only moving a little, building up momentum, but I knew it was a mistake. I clutched him tighter as it moved a little more with each swing, my stomach always just behind, or so it felt. When I opened my eyes next the boat began its first real swing, and the ground swept away, too far away. I screamed into his shoulder and pulled him tight, and then we reached the top. Everything went weightless. The boat swung the other way, and I felt like I was dangling inches above the ground at the other end of the swing, only to sweep *backwards*. Not being able to see made it worse and I jammed my face into his shoulder, hiding.

It was exhilarating. It couldn't have been five minutes, but it felt like we were swinging for an hour. By the time the boat stopped, I was molded against his body and panting. I walked oddly down the exit ramp. He never once let go of my hand, until he settled my hat back on my head.

We took every adult-sized ride in the park. The spinning teacups had me screaming, the helicopter ride had me staring out at the ocean as it carried us high over the park. The only one I refused was the haunted house.

My head still swimming from the pounding I took on the bumper cars, I walked with him down the boardwalk. We ate hotdogs on the way back to the car, and I ate a funnel cake on the way back to school. I broke off pieces and fed them to him as he drove, and shuddered in strange excitement when he lightly licked powdered sugar from my fingers. The crispy, sugar dough melted in my mouth, so sweet it made me sick, but I didn't care.

I was so happy, I never once noticed that we were being followed.

Chapter Twelve

Evelyn

It was a Tuesday, in the afternoon, after my introductory math class ended. The work was trivial. I barely paid attention. My tutors did a masterful job of preparing me.

My phone rang.

"Evelyn," my father said.

"Hello, Father," I said, cheerfully. "How are you?"

"Shut up," he growled. "Walk back to your dormitory. Now."

He hung up.

I almost dropped the phone. My fingers were trembling. Victor would be over after classes to pick me up. If Father saw us together…

He was waiting for me. I knew it. My feet moved on their own. I drifted out of the lecture hall and down the hall, then outside. Then, I saw him. He was standing on the sidewalk in front of my dormitory building. After a quick glance to either side, I rushed across the street and walked up to him, clutching books to my chest.

"Hello, Father." I said, warily. "I need to…"

"Get in the car."

He was parked illegally in the street. I went over anyway and got in, my temples pounding as I waited for him to get in. He started driving.

"Victor is here and you've been seeing him socially."

"He took me to the beach," I murmured, in a very small voice.

"To the movies, to the park. You see him almost every day."

"Yes." There was no point in lying. He would know. He always knew.

"What do you do with him?"

His hands tightened on the steering wheel. I clutched the books harder to my chest. "I… I don't want to talk about it."

"Has he fucked you yet?"

The question was like a slap to the face, like cold water dumped on my head.

"What?"

"You heard me."

"That… I…

I hadn't slept with him. Not yet, but when he spoke like that, Father was at his angriest. I tried to sink through the seat and disappear.

"You're coming with me."

"Where?"

"Home. I'll make arrangements for you to transfer to another school. Had I known the boy transferred here I would have taken care of it already. I'll send someone to gather your things. We're leaving. Now."

"No."

He slammed on the brakes and stopped the car. "What did you say?"

"I said *no,*" I snapped back at him. "I like it here. I like Victor. He's fun. I have fun with him."

"You're not here to have *fun.*"

"You're not paying for this. I earned the scholarship."

I reached for the door. He hit the power locks. I popped the lock and he seized my arm in a vice grip, yanked me back into the seat and floored the gas, throwing me back.

"You can't!" I screamed, "You *can't!*"

He slapped me.

It knocked me back in the seat. I covered my mouth. My fingers came away stained with a hint of red from my split lip. I didn't even feel the pain.

I let out a low whine as the tears started to flow.

"*Stop that,*" he snarled. "How many times do I have to teach you to keep your emotions under control? You're a girl. If someone sees you crying you'll be destroyed. You have to be ice, Evelyn. Ice."

"I don't want to be ice. I want to go home."

"We are."

"Not with you."

The steering wheel creaked under his fingers. "I will tolerate this for now. You'll come to understand after you calm down and we have a chance to talk. After I speak with Karen and Victor leaves, you might be allowed to come back here. I can understand your wishes to stay. I'd rather you graduated from my alma mater as well, but-"

"No. *No.* You are not going to take him away from me."

"He's your stepbrother, Evelyn. It's unseemly, and I already have..."

"Have what?"

"Nothing. Nevermind. Be quiet. It's a long ride and I'd rather not listen to your inane chatter the entire way."

I was going to say something else when a white shape rocketed past his side of the car. Victor's Firebird blasted past us and her tires shrieked as Victor wrestled the wheel around. The car bucked on its springs as he came to a stop across the road. Father slammed on the brakes again, stopping short. He turned the wheel sharply and hit the gas, trying to drive around, but Victor rolled forward, blocking his path. He leapt out of the Firebird and ran around the back, threw open the trunk and pulled out the longest, heaviest wrench I'd ever seen. It was as long as his forearm and looked like it weighed twenty pounds. To my utter shock, Jennifer was in the passenger's seat. She got out as well, following Victor.

"Out of the car," he bellowed, in a voice that shook the windows.

The wrench bobbed in his hand.

I wasted no time. I ripped the door lock open and spilled out, dropping my books in the process. I ran around and behind Victor. I clung to his back with my arms around him.

Father stepped out of the car.

"Evelyn," he said, calmly. "Get back in the car."

"No," I spat at him. "I won't."

"You heard her," said Victor. "Now kindly fuck off."

Father was livid. He bared his teeth, and turned redder by the second.

Jennifer took my arm. "Come on. I'll get your books."

"She's my daughter," Father said.

"This is how it works," said Victor. "You stay the fuck away from her or I have a long, detailed conversation with my mother."

Father's face was a frozen mask. His bright blue eyes burned almost as brightly as my nightmare. He didn't move.

"Get in your car, old man, and I don't bash your brains out."

I tensed, clutching Victor.

"Don't hurt him."

"Hurt him?" Father snorted. "I wouldn't worry about that, Evelyn. Get over here. We're leaving."

"No. I'm staying."

"You heard her," Jennifer added. "Leave."

He didn't, not until the sound of sirens rose in the distance. Then he walked over and got in the car, and nearly backed over my textbooks. He tossed my messenger bag on the ground, did a quick turn, and drove off in the opposite direction. Victor scooped up my things while Jennifer led me back to the car and crawled in the back seat. Victor got in and let out a deep breath, turned the car around and drove down a side street, back towards the college.

"Jesus," He said. His hands were shaking like leaves.

"How did you know?"

"Victor came to the room looking for you," Jennifer said, quietly. "I told him I saw you get in the car with him and Victor freaked out. That's your father?"

"Yes," I said, softly. I was starting to shake.

"We're going to talk to campus security," Victor said, calmly. "I don't want him around here."

Jennifer cleared her throat.

"Can you drop me off?"

"Yeah," Victor said. "Listen, Martin Ross is bad news. If you see him around, call somebody. Stay with other people. You shouldn't be involved in this at all."

"I couldn't just let him drive off with her," said Jennifer. "I should have gone outside when I saw, but..." she trailed off.

"Thank you," I said, turning to her.

We let her off out front of the dorm, and Victor sat there until she was inside before he drove off.

I buried my face in his shoulder and cried.

"You should stay with me tonight. I have my own room."

I swallowed, hard. "Is that a good idea?"

"I'm not going to pressure you to sleep with me."

"That's... that's not what I meant, I didn't mean it like that, I..."

"I didn't mean it like that, either. Stay with me, Eve."

"Okay."

"Let's get something to eat."

We drove out to a pizza place on the highway and ate there, split a medium with sausage and pepperoni between us. I don't know how Victor stayed in such amazing shape, eating the way he did. I felt calmer after I had some food, but I was still rattled and felt like someone was watching me as I tucked some clothes into my smallest bag and told Jennifer she had the room to herself that night. Victor parked the car while I was inside and met me out front, and walked with me across campus to the upperclassmen's dormitories. His room was bigger than the one I shared with Jennifer. There was an extra bed. He had it taken apart and stacked up in the closet. After I came in, he started pulling out, meaning to put it together for me.

"You don't have to do that," I said. My voice was calm, but my body was in turmoil. My stomach was doing backflips, my heart was pounding.

I curled upon his bed without asking and took out a geography textbook. I had to study for class the next day.

The words danced on the page. I suddenly didn't care much for arid and semi-arid lands.

Victor sat down next to me and I closed the book. Gently, he took it from my hands and set it on the other end of the bed. He put his arm around me and I leaned on him, sighing deeply.

"Say what you want, when you're ready."

I didn't know what to say for a long time.

When I finally blurted something out, it was just there.

"I wish I had a mom like yours."

Victor was quiet. I laid down with him, curled up against his side. He didn't press me or say anything. He just let me lay on his arm and rested his hand on my hip.

"I want my mom," I choked out, my voice tight with anguish.

"It still hurts," he said, finally. "I miss my father every day of my life. I'd give up the house and the car and everything else to have him back."

"I thought everyone was like me," I said. "I thought everyone's father was like mine. Jennifer told me about her father. He died not long ago."

Victor nodded.

"He never hit her. He took her and her sister to the beach. He bought them candy and ice cream and he never hit her with a belt or burned her. She could watch TV and read whatever she wanted and she went to school."

It just poured out of me.

"I don't know how to be a person. All I know is math and history I had to memorize. I don't know what to do or what to say about anything. I don't…"

I trailed off, and wept softly.

Victor rolled onto his side to face me and took me in both arms. I wept softly in to his chest for what felt like hours.

"This is a co-ed building. You can get cleaned up in the girl's bathroom if you want."

I nodded, but I didn't want to go anywhere. Victor gave me a washcloth and I cleaned up my face. My eyes were red and puffy and raw and my lip split when my father hit me.

"If he ever hits you again, I swear I will kill him."

I tensed. "You can't. Victor, you can't."

"Just because he's your father-"

"They'd take you away," I said. "I can't lose you, too."

"Eve," he murmured, embracing me from behind.

I leaned back into him.

"You always know how to make me feel better. Make me feel better."

I felt him tense up now.

"Eve, what do you mean?"

I turned around, feeling his arms slip around me. I chewed my bottom lip and unbuttoned the top of my shirt. Victor's eyes went wide but he said nothing. He leaned back and I straddled him, sitting up a little, leaning on his chest with one hand while I undid the buttons with the other. I was not terribly proud of my body and my hand shook so much by the time I was halfway down that I couldn't work the buttons. I took Victor's hand instead and guided him.

"Please," I said.

I sat up as he spread the top over my shoulders and tugged the sleeves free of my arms. I wasn't dressed for seduction, and there was nothing sexy about the plain white t-shirt bra I was wearing, but his rough warm hands were shockingly gentle as he pulled the straps down my shoulders and reached behind me, sitting up a little, to unclasp it. My heart pounded as he pulled it away and drank me in with his eyes. His hands cupped my breasts, and he circled his thumbs lightly around my nipples. It was a hard shock, and made my legs jerk as I sucked in a breath. He sat up and pulled me to him, and kissed me and kept kissing me for what felt like hours, his hands pressed to my back. Finally he rolled onto his side, lowering me to the bed, and tugged my jeans down, took off my shoes and socks.

The more of my skin was exposed, the faster my heart began to beat. I could barely speak by the time he was slowly drawing my panties down my thighs.

"Oh wow," he said.

The hair between my legs was darker than on my head, but not much.

"You look like you're made of silver," he said.

I didn't think so. I thought I was pudgy in my legs and my breasts were too small and my skin too pale, a roadmap of veins all over me growing brighter as I got cold, and gooseflesh popped up all over my skin.

"You're cold," he said, "Here."

He pulled his blankets over me, tucked them up to my neck and stood up. His shirt came off first. I pulled the blankets to my chin and watched, feeling a fluttery feeling in my stomach and heat between my legs. He turned around to undress. The wings tattooed on his back flexed as he moves. He shoved his jeans down and stepped out of them, and I stared at the heavy muscle of his ass and legs. I thought I should be scared, but I wasn't. It was a kind of nervous excitement, a lot like that moment when I realized the boat ride was going to be a lot more intense than he told me it would be. When he turned around, I gasped. I tried not to look at his cock, but it was the first place my eyes went. I was aware of the basic facts of human reproduction but… I'd never seen a man naked before. I didn't know it was supposed to be big like that.

He slipped under the bed and I froze as he put his arms around me. I only relaxed when he kissed me, before he did anything else.

"First time, isn't it?"

I nodded.

"Okay," he said.

His hands were light on my shoulders. He turned me on my back and kissed me. I reached for him, moving my hand down his stomach, but he pulled both my wrists to my sides and continued to kiss me lightly until I closed my eyes. Then he moved lower, touching his lips to my throat in quick, warm touches.

"Victor," I murmured. "I can't get pregnant."

"Don't worry about that yet," he said. "Just relax."

I was trembling, trying my best to relax. He settled on the bed, one arm over my stomach, and spent a very long time softly kissing my throat. He was letting me get used to him. After a while I did begin to relax, even if I was still excited. He had his eyes closed as he worked lower, his mouth and tongue on the skin over my collarbone as his hands caressed my sides. I slipped my arm around his neck and pushed him lower, and he obliged, working his way between my breasts. I never realized how sensitive the skin was there. I started to swear as he worked his mouth around the bottom of my breast from the center of my chest out, his stubbly cheeks scratching my skin, his hot breath flood over me. My nipple stiffened and I thought he would take it in his mouth, but he stopped. I opened my eyes and watched him kiss me everywhere *but* there, cupping my breasts in his hands.

When he finally closed his lips around my nipple I thought I was going to explode. The need between my legs was hot and strong, pulsing down to my toes. I tugged on his hair and pulled on him but he was in control, savoring my body. When he worked further down my stomach, it was like nothing I'd ever felt before. I'd fumbled with my fingers, felt some pleasure in my bed, but I was terrified of myself, in a way. Victor wasn't. He settled in between my legs, kissing his way down from my navel and then I felt his mouth, hot and wet, and his tongue on my sex, and let out a soft sound before clamping my hand down over my mouth. Victor looked up at me, clearly amused at my embarrassment. Then he returned to tasting of my body, lightly at first, then more and more forcefully, his hands sliding down my sides to cup my backside in his hands.

I spread on the bed, my eyes lidded. My hand fell away from my mouth and I gripped the sheets. I started to shake and quiver, my legs, trembling, and Victor backed off, lightly kissing my thighs instead. I relaxed even more, closing my eyes all the way, and he went back to my sex, only this time I felt something press at me. His finger. He was putting his finger inside me. Lightly, experimentally. My slick walls gripped his finger as he entered me, slowly, his hand trembling a little. Deeper, deeper. He was watching me, listening, and when his finger pressed in the right spot and my back arched, he knew he had me. It wasn't long. Each time I lifted to a new height of pleasure I thought it was the end, but there was more. I was drowning in my own body, sliding away into a haze, and then it grew more intense, more powerful, building and building until I arched on the bed and my legs shot out, the muscles clenching and bunching as my throbbing sex squeezed his finger. Suddenly his licking and sucking was too intense and I writhed under him until he stopped, and rolled onto my side, panting.

He sat up and licked his fingers clean.

I though his cock was big before, but it was fully hard now. When he sat up it stood up straight against his belly. I looked at it and thought *he's going to put that inside me*.

He ran his hand over my back. "Feel better?"

"Mmm. Yes."

"Good."

"Are we going to do it?"

"Rest. You're not ready yet."

I swallowed. "I want to something for you."

"Eve," he said.

I was already slipping to the floor. My legs trembled as I knelt beside the bed. I don't know why I was so fascinated with the idea, but looking at his body just made me feel… almost greedy. There was no other word for it. I slipped between his legs and he stared at me, his tight stomach quivering. I rose up on my knees and pressed against him, so his cock pressed against me as I kissed his chest. His skin tasted salty. He was hard all over, but the skin on his chest and stomach were not like I expected, silky smooth. Even the tattoos. Up close, I studied them. There was an urgency in his body, like he was willing me to move lower. As I slid down his cock slid against my body, between my breasts. I dipped down and trembled at the idea, willing myself to do it, psyching up. I dipped down and took his cock in my mouth, and he moaned softly, digging his fingers into my hair. His legs pressed against my arms and he leaned forward over me, panting.

Just the touch of my lips on the head was driving him wild. It made my heart pound in my chest. I took him deeper, ran my tongue around him. I thought he would like it if I used to my hand, too, so I did, and he gripped the edge of the bed with one hand while knotting his fingers in my hair with the other. His body trembled and his hips rocked as I moved my head up and down, testing him. I could feel the tension building in his body with every stroke, every touch. When I made a soft, hungry little sound, he tensed up all over, the head of his cock flaring in my mouth. I sucked on the tip and stroked the shaft, my spittle making it slippery in my hand. Victor tensed and tensed, his whole body shaking. Veins stood out on his stomach, and as I cupped his balls in my hand I felt them tighten.

He cried out like he was in pain, his face tight and red and sweaty, but it wasn't pain. There was a hot, explosive rush in my mouth and I didn't know what else to do but swallow, so I did. Then there was more, and more, and more. I felt strange, possessive and possessed at the same time.

I sat back, kneeling on the floor, staring at his cock, then at him. He put his hands under my arms and pulled me up onto the bed with him, and to my surprise, kissed me. He rolled on top of me and kept kissing me, holding me in his arms. I wanted him inside me.

"I want to have sex," I said, leaning on him.

I rolled on my back.

He rolled on his side and put his arms around me. Victor kissed me, and I curled my hand around his cock until he stiffened again. He had condoms in his dresser. He showed me how to put it on him, and I lay on my back, trembling.

"Relax," He murmured as he slid on top of me.

"It's a lot bigger than your finger," I whispered.

"I know. I'm not going to hurt you. If you want to stop, tell me. Are you sure you-"

"Yes."

I thought he would stay on top of me, but he didn't. He rolled over and took me with him. Suddenly I was lying on his chest, resting on my arms. I sat up, gripping his hips with my thighs. I took his shaft in my hand and rubbed the tip against my entrance, feeling the warm. I'd been wet before, but not like this. It was sticky on my legs and I was throbbing, my body insistent. I shifted my weight and pressed him against me and all of a sudden he was inside, just a bit. I made an awkward noise and he held my sides to steady me. It felt so strange. He was *big*. I sank down on him slowly, shaking the whole time, until I settled in his lap and he sat up a bit, and pulled me towards him. I felt so weird with the heavy mass of him inside me, spreading me open, moving as I moved. He wrapped his arms around me lightly and moved under me, and I collapsed on top of him, overwhelmed by the sensation.

Slowly, he rolled on top of me. I closed my legs around him and he strained against me, his face buried in my hair. On top of me, he made me feel small, but I liked it. I thought it was supposed to hurt. My books always talked about how it hurt. This didn't hurt. It felt better than anything. He kissed me, murmured in my ear, laughed when I let out cries of pleasure. He slowed and stopped, and drew out of me. I was confused and started to ask if he was done, but he touched my lips with his finger and moved on the bed so he lay behind me, and slid back into me from behind. It was easier this time. My body just took him all at once, and I moaned at the feeling of completeness. His hand moved between my legs and he lightly stroked my clit while he pumped into me from behind and it drove me wild. I had to pull his hand away as my sex began throbbing, squeezing his shaft as he drove into me.

I felt it when he finished in me. I tugged on his wrist as he used his fingers on me, my body clenching on him as he drove me to a second peak, a shaking, earth-shattering shock that passed through me in waves, from my toes to my scalp. When it was over he gently drew out of me but laid there holding me, one hand between my legs, the other lightly cupping my breast, his face buried in my hair. He breathed deep, taking in my scent, his chest flexing against my back. He pulled the blankets up over my shoulder.

"How was it?"

"I liked it," I panted. "Can we do it again tomorrow?"

I wish I could just stop it all right there. Freeze time.

Chapter Thirteen

Evelyn

It is beginning to rain. It drums on the windshield. Alicia hasn't said a word since I started talking. I told her things I'd never told anyone else, never spoken aloud. I stare through the windshield as the rain turns into streaks. It's getting dark.

"How long were you together?" she says, finally.

"All though college. Three years."

Her hands drum on the steering wheel. "It sounds like you were a completely different person."

"What makes you say that?"

"The girl you just told me about was naive. Sheltered. A guy like Victor must have seen you coming a mile away. How did he hurt you?"

"I don't want to talk about that," I snap. "So what am I like now?"

She's quiet for a time. She sighs.

"You're like him."

"Like Victor?"

"No. You're like your father."

I should be angry that she said that, but I'm not. My arms slide around my body and I hug myself.

"He was right," I say softly. "He wasn't right to hit me. He shouldn't hit me."

"Then we need to stop him."

I roll right over her. "He was right about everything else. He was right about Victor. I thought he cared about me. I thought he needed me. He just used me. I was just another plaything for him. He used me until he was bored with me and then balled me up and threw me away, like a used tissue. The things I did for him, the things I said for him, and everything he said to me was a lie."

"What lie?"

I scrub at my eyes with a napkin. It's starting to turn into little pills, tearing apart from being scrubbed against my skin.

"There was another girl. After me. She worked for the company. His company. He was fucking her while he was still sleeping with me." My voice goes as tight as a stretched piece of rubber, ready to snap. "I thought he was going to ask me to marry him. I wanted him to. I never felt about anyone the way I felt about him. Nobody ever made me feel that way. I would have done anything for him. Anything. He had me wrapped around his finger. I wasn't enough. He wanted more. Her name was Brittany," I spat, bitterly.

"How do you know he was having an affair with her?"

I look over at her.

"I saw pictures."

"Of them having sex?" Alicia blurts out.

"No. Coming and going together."

"What did Victor say about it?"

"He tried to hide it from me. I heard it from her, too. We all did. Me. His mother. My father. In court."

Alicia blinks a few times. "The trial. When they sent him to prison."

"Yes," I sigh. "The trial. That was the last straw. When I listened to her describing the *nature of their relationship*, something cracked inside me." I touch my chest, showing her where. "No. Not cracked. Something inside me hardened. Turned to stone. To ice. I understood all of it. I knew why he was so harsh, why he sheltered me. This world is pointless and cruel. We're cursed with these *feelings*, these *needs*, but all they are is a way for other people get under our skin and use us and exploit us."

Somehow I manage to say all of that without realizing I'm sobbing.

Her hand rests on my back.

"Oh honey, that's not true at all."

"How do you know?"

"I've been married for fifteen years," she sighs. "I'm not going to lie to you. It does hurt. A lot. Maybe even most of the time. But when it doesn't , those times are worth it. You told me about going to that park and all the time you spent with him and you were happy. Would you give that back to get rid of the pain? Erase it all so you don't have to feel this anymore?

I shake my head.

"I didn't think so. Did you ever give him a chance to explain himself?"

"What is there to explain? My father was right. All he cared about was fucking me. He probably thought it was funny, or it excited him to break some silly rule about sleeping with me because our parents are married. It has to be true. It has to."

"Why?"

My hands shake in front of me and my jaw trembles. I can barely choke the words out.

"If I'm wrong, all this time he's been in prison and if he didn't do anything wrong... what if I hated him all this time and he didn't do it? What then? All that time is gone. Ripped away, and I... I never..."

"What?"

I can't take it. I pound my fists on her dashboard.

"His mom made me promise," I cry out, sobbing. "She was dying and she was in the hospital and she made me promise to tell him, to give him a chance but I couldn't do it, I couldn't go and I never told him what she said. I never told him."

I curl up for a bit, just breathe. Try to keep my food down.

"She got sick when he got in trouble," I rasp. "It was like it just broke something in her. The evidence was too damning. If it was just my father she might not have believed, *I* might not have believed, but when they came to arrest him, when they had the trial. It has to be true. He was embezzling from the company, stealing money. He was tied up in all these awful illegal things, they had proof. That had his signature on things, pictures of him coming and going, all the witnesses. I *hate* him. He ruined me. He ruined everything."

"Doesn't matter how many times you keep saying you hate him, honey. It's not any more true now than it was before."

I flinch.

"I saw how you two looked at each other in that office. Neither of you hates the other one."

"I have to know the truth."

"Yeah. I think you do. What should we do?"

"Get me out of here. Drive, I don't care where."

She nods and starts driving while I slump in the seat. I pull up the hood of my sweatshirt and fold my arms around myself, and stare through the streaked windows. It hurts so much. I just want to disappear.

"You still have a chance, you know," she says.

I don't answer her.

"How old are you? Twenty-eight? Honey, you're not even thirty. Your life isn't over."

"Sometimes I wish it was. How many people have I hurt?"

"Not every company you take over gets shut down. Lots of people kept their jobs because of-"

"I haven't run a single takeover that didn't end up cutting jobs." The traffic lights become baleful glows in the mist. I lean on my hand. "I order staff reductions…" I trail off. "I fired people to improve bottom lines."

"Right. If you tried to keep everybody, they'd go under and they'd all lose their jobs."

"I read those tweets, Alicia. "How many people's Christmases have I ruined? How many divorces have I caused? I never even thought about it before. All I saw was numbers in a spreadsheet, charts and projects and equations. It's like I forgot people existed."

"How many Christmas presents did you ever get?"

I look over at her. She's still not looking at me. "What?"

"How many?"

"It's not like I counted them."

"Fine. How many from your father?"

"None. We didn't celebrate holidays at my house. Father said it was frivolous and I could buy what I wanted with my allowance. If I needed something there was no reason to wait until December twenty-fifth to buy it for me."

"What about Victor and his mother?"

"They had huge Christmases. Father hated it. I could tell. He accepted gifts and bought things for Victor's mother, anyway. She and Victor gave me things. He gave me jewelry and…" I feel myself blush.

Alicia's eyebrow quirks up. "And?"

"Other things. Sexy underwear."

"People call it 'lingerie', Eve."

"Whatever," I say, sullenly. "What am I going to do?"

"I don't know."

"What would you do?"

"I'd hear what Victor had to say."

"He hates me now."

"No, he does not. You sound like a twelve year old. Didn't you hear what I told you? That man was not looking at someone he hated. He wanted to take you with him. He wasn't there to

222

hurt you, Eve. He was there to rescue you, even if he doesn't know it."

"I don't know how to reach him."

Alicia sighs. "I can find out. It is my job. Where's there a place where you could meet him?"

"Far away from here. If I do this, Father will find out."

"Find out, and hit you again, you mean."

I flinch.

"It's a ways from here. It's a drive. We should go get one of the cars."

"No, we'll take mine," Alicia says.

I'm not used to being contradicted. It's a long drive. First, we stop at the house. Alicia goes inside and comes back with a bag of my clothes, puts them in the back of her van. I listen while she talks to her husband, who is displeased that she isn't coming home tonight, at the very least. Their conversation is so *domestic*. I curl up in the seat and hug myself and Alicia drives, and drives, and drives. It's almost a three hour trip, all in silence. City gives way to suburbs, suburbs give way to open fields and the swampy hinterlands of the Delmarva peninsula. By the time we arrive I've been asleep for an hour and it's almost dark. One of the advantages of my wealth is I don't have to worry about the cost of booking a room, but in November all the fine waterfront hotels are closed. Alicia takes the company card and books two rooms, one for each of us.

I sprawl out on the bed of a Motel 8 and stare at the popcorn ceiling as if the tiny little swirls and bumps could give me some kind of answers. Alicia is in the other room, making phone calls.

Just past midnight, there's a knock at the door. Wearily, I get up and trudge over, and pull it open. I expect Alicia.

Victor stands in the door, soaked to the bone from the driving rain that kicked up while I was lying on the bed in half-sleep. Water has glued his thick black hair to his head and drips from the tip of his nose, but he holds his head high like it's nothing and stares at me with his clear, piercing eyes.

"Hello," I say, softly. "Come in."

I step back. He walks into the room and sloughs off a rain soaked jacket onto the floor, takes a towel from the bathroom and dries his face. The rain slashes the windows, drums on the heater built into the wall beside the door. I bolt the door and slide the chain lock into place and stand there, trying to make my hands stop shaking, but I can't.

"Your assistant called me," he says, dully. "She says you want to talk. Said to meet you here."

"Yes. I want to talk."

I sit down on the edge of the bed, facing him, but I can't look at him. Just seeing him stirs up all these emotions, like a storm brewing inside me.

"What did you want to talk about?"

I swallow. "Victor."

He's still silent. His eyes are hard.

"Do you hate me?"

He doesn't answer.

I pull my legs up under me and fold them, and hug myself. I still can't look at him. "When your mother was in the hospital, she made me promise to pass a message to you, but I never did." I'm surprised how even my voice is. "She told me to tell you she was wrong, and you were right, about everything. She told me to tell you she believed you were innocent."

"Is that all she said?"

"Yes."

"That doesn't make her any less dead, Eve. She died while I was in prison. I wasn't allowed to see her."

I swallow. "She asked me something else."

"What?"

"She asked me to give you a chance. To hear you out."

"What makes you think I should hear you out?"

My eyes snap up to look at him. The words are like a dagger in my chest.

"I thought…"

"I gave you everything, Eve, and the first time we were tested, you believed the worst about me and wouldn't let me defend myself."

"Your reputation preceded you."

His teeth pull back in a sneer and his fists clench. "That ended with you, Eve. I never touched another girl since I met you."

"She said-"

"She *lied*," he snaps, and pounds his fist on his thigh.

I flinch and his expression softens.

"I didn't mean to scare you, but God damn it, Eve. It makes me mad. I'm angry with you."

"Do you hate me?"

"No. Not you. Never you."

"I'll hear you out, if you want to talk to me."

He gets up and walks to the window. "Why'd you come here?"

"We were always happy here."

"We never stayed at this motel."

I roll my eyes. "I don't mean here, here. I mean at the beach. I still remember that first trip. I was like a little kid. Nobody ever did anything like that for me before, ever."

"It was always fascinating to watch," he says, watching the rain streak the window. "Everything was new to you. Little things brought you such joy. Cotton candy and stuffed animals and the silly little rides at that park."

"Funland," I correct.

"Funland."

"I know now why Father wouldn't let me see you."

"Wouldn't let you?"

"He kept me away at first. After a while he didn't have to. I stayed away on my own. When I saw you what, yesterday? It was…"

"You said you'd hear me out."

"Yes."

"So stop talking, and hear me."

I slide back up the bed to sit against the wall. Victor continues to stare out the window.

"I was never happier than when I was with you. You know, I became a real son of a bitch after I lost my father. The way only a twelve year old can be. I was a little shit to my mother. I hurt a lot of girls. Emotionally, I mean. Not physically. Then when you were around it didn't *hurt* anymore. Not like it used to. It wasn't so bad, and the more you were around the better I felt. I started to think I could have a future with you. The other shit never really mattered to me. I guess I didn't know how well off I had it. The money and the house and all didn't matter to me. It was just there."

I look at his reflection. His eyes are distant, locked on nothing.

"Five years," he said. "Five years with nothing but time. I could have survived that, if I thought you'd be waiting for me. I thought I'd lost you permanently. I thought you'd been poisoned against me. I thought he *won*. Nothing was worse than that."

"I'm sorry," I say, dully.

"If you'd believed me," he sighs. "No, it doesn't matter. I was going down no matter what. I was so stupid. He set me up. Your father. It was a trap and I fell for it, hard. Completely. He beat me."

"Tell me what happened. The truth. All of it."

He turns from the window and falls into a side chair. His hair is still wet when he slides his hand through it. In short sleeves, the feathery tattoos on his arms shiver. I remember being wrapped in those arms, tracing my fingernails over those designs. My touch excited him. Would it excite him now, or disgust him? When he sees me biting my lip his nostrils flare and his whole posture changes. A little quiver of fear flutters through me, flavored with excitement. He looks away, his jaw set.

"You want the truth?" he says, and his voice never wavers. "I love you. That's the truth."

"What about the girl?"

Brittany. Her name is Brittany. I won't say it, I won't give it voice.

"She was lying."

"About the sex, or all of it?"

"All of it. I should have seen it coming. I was set up."

"You said. Set up how?"

"Your father played me," he says, coldly. "Played on my one weakness, too. He was very smart about it."

"What weakness?" I'm about to say *redheads* but I bite my tongue.

"The possibility of freeing you from him forever. I thought I had a shot at taking him down. This is what happened."

Chapter Fourteen

Victor

I never knew what happiness was until I woke up with Evelyn in my arms. When she slept she would curl up in a ball and press against me, the tip of her nose pressed into my chest, the soft feathery touch of her breath on my skin. She always tucked her arms under mine and half the time she'd throw a leg over me, too, like she was trying to wrap me up so I couldn't get away. It was our third year together. Soon I would be graduating from college. She had another year if she chose to continue her studies. I was pushing her to declare a new major. She could do whatever she wanted and I'd pay for it. She didn't need her father's approval, and she didn't need *him*. I had her, I would take care of her. This was the best day of my life. The school year would end soon. We'd decided that after sneaking around for the last two summers we'd be open this year. Eve was ready to confront her father.

Once I graduated, everything would be mine. All of it. The company, the house, the estate, the fortune.

The first thing I was going to do was accept Martin Ross' resignation from the position my mother had secured for him. I'd make sure Mom was well taken care of. If she wanted to take care of her husband in turn, that was her business. I hadn't spoken with her about it yet, but I think she knew. She refused to believe me about the abuse, and I couldn't very well tell her I'd spent hours with Eve with both of us in the nude, tracing the ridged scars on her back. I never imagined he'd left *permanent marks* on her until she disrobed for me in the light for the first time. I wasn't sure what the marks were that first night when it was dark in the room and she wouldn't come out from under the covers. When I saw, I knew. Scars. From the edge of a belt biting into her skin. They were old and faded, just lines in the way old scars are, but that's what they were. He'd whipped her until she bled.

I wanted to kill him. Twist his head right off his skinny little neck. For Eve's sake, I didn't. I'd just send him far away from her and keep her for myself. I won. I saved the virgin princess from the monster. In a couple of months everything would be perfect.

We'd even talked about the idea of children a few times. Not really talked, like a serious conversation, but once in a while one or the other of us would drop a line about the kids we were going to have, here or there.

Eve stirred next to me. I always woke up first. I liked watching her sleep. She looked so peaceful with her head pillowed on my arm, her pale hair tousled around the bed. Her eyes fluttered open and she stretched, and put her arms around my neck. Bare under the sheets, she pressed her chest to mine. Her nipples were hard and it wasn't from the cold. Late March, so it was cold in the room but we were piled up in blankets. She had a roommate and a dorm of her own but she might as well have lived with me. Her hands slipped under the covers and I rolled her onto her back and kissed her. She giggled into my mouth and wrapped her fingers around my cock. I was already hard for her, I woke up ready as usual. After our first few months together we were committed, so she went on the pill and we stopped using protection.

Nothing was so sweet as entering her. Eve was wet and ready, her hot silky walls gripping me as I moved on top of her and entered her in a slow, gradually building thrust that made her let out an anxious, throaty moan that ended in a breathy little gasp. She was shivering and there was gooseflesh on her arms, so I pulled the blankets up a round our necks and warmed her with my breath. She felt so small and fragile beneath me, delicate in a way that made me move slowly, savor the sensations of moving inside her. Every gentle thrust made me shudder, and then she dug her heels into my thighs and urged me on, faster, harder. She only seemed fragile, it was an illusion. She'd been whipped into something harder than that. When it's cold enough, ice is harder than steel. Eve melted in my arms, but the strength didn't.

Her nails clawed into my back and she bit my shoulder. It stung, it *hurt*, and it only made me want her more. Rocking the whole bed with my movements. She slid her arms around my neck and bucked her hips under me.

I rolled onto my back, taking her with me. It felt so fucking good when her weight pressed her down in my lap, driving my shaft deep inside her. She sat up and let the blankets fall away, and wriggled her hips in a circle, eyes closed, biting her lip in concentration. Eve had confessed to me that she thought she was ugly. I had no idea where that idea came from. She thought her nose was too long and sharp, I thought it was cute. She thought she had a weasely face, I thought she looked like some exotic fox. She thought her hair was dull and lifeless, I thought it was like burnished silver and felt like silk. She thought it was ugly the way the veins stood out under her skin when she was cold, tracing a road map across her skin. I thought it made her beautiful and strange. I held her by the ribs as she moved her hips in rolling thrusts, her face pinching in an adorable mask of pleasure as she rode me.

Eve doubled forward and I grabbed her hips to stop her movement, made her go still. She sat on me with my cock buried inside her until I gently pushed her off and rolled her onto her side, and pressed against her back. I guided myself inside her from behind, lying against her, and cupped her breasts in my hands and buried my face in her sweet smelling hair. She smelled like lilacs, from her favorite shampoo, and she smelled like Eve. There is no other smell like that. Eve just smells like Eve. I moved one hand down her stomach, slowed my own movements. It was agony to hold back. By now I knew her body perfectly. She grasped my wrist in one hand, clasped the other to her chest over mine. With my cock inside her and my fingers working her stiff little clit, she started to pant and tighten up almost instantly, her moans turning into little squeaks as she squeezed my wrist. I started to thrust harder as I could feel her getting close, let myself go. It was tough to time it this way but I had practice. When she started to shudder and her body tensed like coiled springs I knew it was coming. She was so hot and tight. I wrapped my arms around her body and exploded inside her as she thrashed against me, kicking her little feet, bucking in my arms, the little noises she made almost pained. After a while she went limp, lying sideways on the bed. I didn't draw out of her.

"I have a class," she sighed.

"When?"

'Ten."

"It's nine. Let's do it again."

She smiled softly and disentangled herself from my arms.

I had a suite to myself in the upperclass dorm. I could afford it, after all. That meant I had my own bathroom and was treated to the sight of Eve traipsing naked through the room to pluck a cleanish towel from the pile by the bathroom door and step inside. She started the shower and steam poured through the door. Eve liked hot showers more than anything. After lying there for a few minutes to catch my breath I got up and followed her in, slipped into the shower behind her and started soaping up her back. She had her hair in a wet cord, thrown over her shoulder. After she stood under the water, shivering from the chilly air despite the scalding steam, it was my turn to soap up. She did my back first, and she pressed against me and wrapped her hands lightly around my cock.

"I thought you had class," I said.

"I do, but I don't want to leave you like this."

She pressed her cheek against my back and stroked my cock in her hands. I could almost feel her smiling. It never took her long this way. Soon I was fully hard and not long after that I was leaning on the wall while she quickly, lightly stroked me off. I groaned loudly as I lost in her hand, cupped around the pulsing tip of my shaft. She let the water sluice her hands clean, leaned against me to kiss my cheek, and stepped out.

When I was actually washed up, I stepped out after her. By now she was dressing, already wearing a pair of sweat pants and a bra as she dried her hair. I went over and flopped on the bed. I had no classes until noon. Eve pulled on a t-shirt and then a hoodie I gave her last year. She always left so damned early for class, but she liked to be the first one in the room for whatever reason. I stood up to kiss her before she left, and gave her butt a squeeze while I was at it. She giggled and batted my hand away and gave me a look that said *later*, and then she was off.

I sprawled out on the bed and watched the clock. Around eleven I got up for real, after half-dozing for an hour or so, thinking about having

Eve again. I rose, put on something halfway presentable, and grabbed my notebooks. Eve practically took a bookstore to class with her. I carried the bare minimum, the notebooks I needed and some pens. I'd take my laptop if I needed it, but I didn't today. It was a *leadership* course, a senior seminar type thing, and I'd spend most of my time listening to the self proclaimed eccentric professor bullshitting. You've met the guy, even if you've never met him specifically. He liked to mention early and often how he was rich running all these companies and quit to be a business professor instead. He assigned a book because he had to and told the students not to buy it, and half the classes were lectures about shoes or TED talks. He liked this one from a guy that got high with a bunch of different cultures. Once in a great while we actually talked about business ethics.

You can imagine how much I was looking forward to *that*. Resigned, I headed out the door. Then my phone rang.

I didn't know the number. I leaned against the wall by the door.

"Hello?"

"Mister Amsel?" a female voice said.

I blinked a few times. "Who's this?"

"My name is Brittany Andrews. I work at the company."

"What company?"

"*Your* company," she said. "I need to talk to you."

"So, talk."

"In person. I'd rather not do this over the phone. I don't feel safe."

I blinked a few times. "Fine. I get out of class this afternoon. I'll pick up my girlfriend and…"

"No. It has to be soon, and alone. This is a big deal, Mister Amsel. I'm scared. I don't know what to do."

"Okay. A public place, then. Where are you, anyway?"

"I'm at work at the company. In Philadelphia."

"It's going to take me over an hour to get there. There's a coffee shop on the corner outside the office."

"Too close. Someone might see me."

"Fine. I know a pizza place on Market street, at third. Right on the corner."

"That will work. I'll be waiting for you."

She hung up on me.

I stared at the phone. This was like some next level spy movie shit. I did have class, but no one would care if I skipped and Eve would gladly help me with the homework from my afternoon class. Still, I'd be gone for a while.

It was a long drive. Eve made me promise to stop getting so many speeding tickets after they threatened to yank my license, so I took it slow and easy. Almost an hour and a half later I was cruising downtown Philly looking for a place to wedge the Firebird into a parking spot. I finally gave up and pulled into a paid lot, and walked down to the pizza place. In the afternoon it had grown warm, t-shirt weather. When I stepped into the pizza place, a woman stood up from a wrought iron table where a half-eaten pepperoni personal pizza sat before her. She saw me and headed over.

I'm going to admit it. She was hot, very hot. Tall, and shapely in a way that shows under conservative business attire. Long legs that looked great in spiked heels, and curly bright red hair in a frizzy ponytail. She had a kind of no makeup look going, and bright green eyes. High cheekbones, a heart shaped face, the works. A few years ago I'd have already been working on getting her number and getting her guard down, but today I shook her hand. Her attractiveness was a quality that I noted, just something that was there. It wasn't something I imposed on myself, it wasn't discipline, it just was. All of a sudden I went from a ladies' man to a man that could only see two women in the world. Eve, and the other ones.

I sat down with her at the table and motioned the waitress over. She brought me a Coke and a healthy pile of boneless wings which I greedily slathered in blue cheese as I ate.

"What's this about?"

Brittany swallowed, hard. She put her hand on mine. I quickly pulled it away and gave her a look.

"It's not like that. I'm sorry," she said. "I'm really scared. I found something I shouldn't have."

"Who are you, exactly?"

"I'm Mister Ross's personal assistant," she said, and swallowed, hard.

Oh, cute. My mother's new husband has a ten-out-of-ten redhead personal assistant. I wonder if he introduced them at the company picnic?

Probably not.

Brittany drummed her fingernails on the cast iron. I chowed down.

"Spit it out," I said, after a choking swallow of Coke. Shit, why did I order the extra hot sauce?

"I found evidence that your stepfather-"

"Martin," I corrected.

"I found evidence that Martin is involved in some shady things. Do you know what a bust out is?"

I shook my head.

"It's a kind of organized crime scheme. The criminals exploit a company by extending its line of credit until it goes bankrupt, then use the money the company borrowed to buy its own assets and resell them, then hand off the bad debt. An extortion scheme, basically."

"Okay. So Martin is involved with this? He's going to bust out Amsel?"

"No, I don't think that's even possible. The company is huge. Do you have any idea what your net worth is?"

"It's my mother's net worth until I graduate, and yes, I have a rough idea."

"Lately the company has been underwriting a lot of mergers and acquisitions. Your father is in charge of them. He has a partner he's working with."

She opened her satchel and slid a folder across the table to me. I wiped hot sauce off my mouth with a napkin and spread the folder open, and sucked down soda to cool the burn. It didn't help.

I read through the file.

"What am I looking at, exactly?"

"Amsel acquired this office supply company last year. Your step… uh, Martin has been channeling funds from the company into his private accounts. See these loans they've taken out?"

"Yeah. I've never heard of this bank before. That's a lot of money."

"I think they're part of the Russian mob."

I gave her an incredulous look and glanced down at the file again. "You're kidding."

"He's been meeting a lot with somebody named Vitali. They went on a yacht cruise together about six months ago."

"He has a yacht?"

"It belongs to this Vitali."

"You have the dates?"

"Yes."

I took a deep breath. "Why'd you come to me? Why not go to the police?"

"Russian. Mafia."

"Right, but what am I supposed to do about this?"

"It's your company. You have pull that I don't. You can go places I don't. I don't have proof here, Mister Amsel. Not iron clad proof that will stand up in court and put these men away. If I go public with this, I'm dead. Martin scares me," she started to choke up. "He's... he's not like other people. He's hollow inside. Dead. I'm nothing to him. He goes through assistants like crazy. I've lasted longer than the last three combined. I should just quit, but this is hurting people. This office supply company has thousands of employees and they're all going to lose their job when the company folds and Amsel sells off the assets. I need access to higher level files and accounts. Access you have. You're not connected to any of this. You're the only person I can trust."

"Okay. Let's go."

"This isn't going to take a few hours, Mister Amsel. It's going to take weeks, months even. We need to be very careful. We can't tell *anyone* about this. Do you understand?"

"Yeah. So what now?"

"I'll be in touch. I have to get back to the office before I'm missed. Look around and make sure nobody is following you."

A few minutes after she left, as I was finishing my chicken, Eve called me.

I had to figure out what I was going to tell her. I wasn't going to be telling her that I was working on sending her father to prison.

Chapter Fifteen

Victor

The company was a weird place to me. No matter how old I was, it was still "going to work with Dad" except there was no Dad to go with me. Everyone knew who I was, though, on sight. I wore a conservative dark suit and tie. The sleeves covered my tattoos. I'd designed them that way, to remain hidden in business attire. When I visited, it raised eyebrows. The Heir didn't often stop by. Maybe once or twice a year. Since I was eighteen I'd been meeting semi-regularly with the management. Amsel is privately held, so no board of directors, only employees. These old men worked for me. I signed in at the front desk. Amsel occupied the top three floors of a center city highrise. The whole building belonged to me, but our offices took up only the three floors. For the most part, when Amsel invested in something, a publicly traded company did the actual work. Amsel itself was only what's called a holding company, owning the stock and directing with a light touch.

For the better part of two hundred years, it worked. Amsel prospered by finding men of talent in fields of interest and funding them. Synthetic fibers, explosives, medicine, chemistry, computers. Most people probably never heard of us until Eve took over the company and started making waves, but Amsel owned a piece of everyone's daily lives, from the food they ate to the clothes they wore to the cars they drove. That's a lot of money, flowing in and out, year after year, day after day, hour after hour. Somewhere I had a calculation to tell me how much money I made while I was using the bathroom. Tuition was meaningless to me. I could have *bought* the college if I felt like it.

There was only one thing that mattered and I was going to lose it.

I showed the receptionist my driver's license and signed in at the front desk, and headed to the elevator. I wanted this tedium to be over. Really, I wanted to just stick my head in the sand and deal with this when I took over. Once it was official and I had my degree, the requirements of my father's will would be satisfied and I would be the sole owner of the company. Then it would be bye bye Martin. As of that moment, my part of the company was held in trust managed by my mother, and my mother put Martin in charge after he managed her portion of the estate successfully for years. That was how they met, years ago now. So far as I knew their marriage was happy. He never laid a hand on my mother and he was hands off with Eve, too, virtually ignoring her during the summers between semesters. We still kept things quiet, leaving the estate when we wanted to spend the night together, but it would take a fool not to realize where we were going and what we were doing.

Fool that I was, I thought we really were keeping it a secret. I was trying to talk Eve into coming off the birth control after I graduated. She wanted to finish her degree. I respected that. She was starting to budge on coming off after she graduated herself, a year from now. That would work for me. Not like we were going to *try* for a kid, so much as let nature take its course. If we kept at it like we had been before, nature would take its course pretty quick. When

I was younger if you told me that I'd be thinking about marriage and kids when I was only twenty-two years old, I'd have been horrified. Now I could barely think of anything else. The idea of filling the halls of that huge sprawling house with children was starting to appeal to me. Mom wanted more kids with Dad, but it never happened and he was gone when she was so young. If he'd lived I'd have brothers and sisters, I know it.

My every instinct was screaming at me to Let. It. Be.

I had to know. If Martin was trying to destroy my family legacy I had to know. I had to be able to take care of Eve.

Arms folded, I leaned on the elevator wall and sighed, waiting for it to ascend. If it was up to me I'd be fixing cars for the rest of my days. Hell, maybe I'd find a manager -anybody but Martin-and do just that. Be hands off. Dad was like that. He came here maybe two days a week, and didn't visit at all for long stretches in the summer. Up until around he died, anyway. Something happened then and he was spending hours every day, but he'd leave super early and be home in the middle of the afternoon to spend time with me and then spend the evenings with Mom. That was a happier time, happier than I can remember until I convinced Eve to take a chance on me.

Eve. If I closed my eyes I could smell that lavender, like tasting a color. I wanted to get this shit over with and get back to her.

I still hadn't told her where I was, what I was doing. She thought I was in class right now. If I made it back in time, nothing would be amiss.

The elevator came to my floor. I stopped in at the receptionist's desk and signed in again. Yes, twice. Just to be on the safe side.

Then I went to meet Brittany.

It didn't feel like I was ruining my life. Every employee that saw me greeted me pleasantly. Old men slapped me on the back and told me it would be good to have an Amsel at the helm again after so long. One even squeezed my arm and told me my father would be proud of me. That made my day. It was a subtle thing.

The record's vault was in the 27th floor, the second floor of the three belonging to the company. That was where I was to meet

Brittany. There was no guard or anything. The big vault door opened with a pass code, a unique one assigned to everyone with access. Lots of important stuff was stored in here, and on paper. There were electronic records but Amsel is old fashioned, it's just how things go. Institutional momentum, my dad called it once. He was talking to my mother when he called it that. I punched in my code and the door popped open with a hollow metal thump and a *hiss* of escaping air.

Brittany was already inside. She dressed conservatively, as usual. Her reading glasses were cute, but I noted it as a passing thing, a simple fact like the color of her gray skirt or the heels on her pumps. She was going for a sexy schoolmarm look, I think. I just wanted to get this over with and get out of there. I closed the vault door and sealed it from the inside.

The implications of this did not come to me at the time. Unfortunately.

She had a lot of paperwork spread out on the reading table in the middle of the room. Some of it was photocopies. Anything older than six months was put on microfilm and the originals destroyed at a secure facility that specialized in that kind of thing. It was tossed in right in boxes and eaten by a huge, scary looking crosscut machine and the cuttings were incinerated. I think the machine was called an Industrial Macerator. Sounds pleasant.

"What am I looking at?" I said, leaning over the papers.

"I started pulling some of the paperwork on the accounts I told you about. Amsel is becoming involved with some very unsavory people."

"Show me."

"Okay," she took a deep breath. "Amsel acquired this office supply company last year. Paperclips."

"They make Paperclips?"

"No, that's the name of the company. Paperclips."

"That's not a very good name."

She sighed. "This is serious, Victor. Here's the kicker," she slipped me a page. "When Amsel acquired a controlling interest in Paperclips, the company was *deep* in the hole. They were a quarter billion in debt. Amsel propped up the company on the standard terms, requiring a reorganization and so on. They started to turn a profit. Then this happens."

She slid me another paper. I picked it up and skimmed it.

"The company bought bonds," I said.

"Right. When you buy bonds, you're basically loaning money. The bond is like a bank note. You turn it in when it matures, get paid back with interest."

"Okay. So?"

"So, Amsel's holdings don't buy bonds. They pay a dividend on stock back to the company itself. To you, basically. They don't lend money out. The company started taking on debt of its own and loaning it back out on these bonds. So I looked into where the bonds were coming from."

She handed me a list. I took it in both hands and skimmed it.

"I've never heard of any of these companies."

"Right, and you wouldn't. They don't exist. They all claim to be chartered in Russia, but none of them are real. I checked. The money is just disappearing up its own ass. Pardon my French."

"Okay then. Now what?"

"Now Paperclips is being shuttered. The company is going into bankruptcy. Amsel owns stock, they... *you* don't actually own the company, so you're basically a creditor. Shielded from the debt. I learned about this two weeks ago when an investigator from the securities and exchange commission showed up. Now, look at this."

She had more paperwork. I read it, but it was just some stock trades. Very good stock trades. Martin made me quite a bit of money on them, even if he was putting me on the hook for fake debt to Russian shell companies.

"What am I looking at?"

"You've been insider trading," she said, sighing.

"I've been *what?*"

"Legally, it's you. Martin manages the account, obviously, so he's on the hook. Someone has been passing him a lot of information. Corporate espionage stuff, mostly, but he got Amsel into the market before a couple of important pharmaceutical industry bills passed. Netted the company hundreds of millions, and a nice commission for himself. The management agreed to give him a sizeable bonus out of the returns. Most of it went to you, of course."

Brittany took the papers and neatly stacked them up.

"What you see here is an orgy of evidence. There's enough stuff here to send Martin to prison for the rest of his life, and the SEC does not, pardon my French, fuck around."

I nodded slowly.

Gotcha.

"Why didn't you go to the authorities yourself?"

"Because of his associates. Martin has been talking to this Vitali person constantly. I don't want end up in pieces in an oil drum somewhere, Mister Amsel. I need protection. Help from somebody who can protect me. Not witness protection or something like that. I don't want to destroy my life."

"Alright. So what do you need from me?"

"I need your access code. There's some stuff I can't get on my own. I was hoping we could go through that now, see what we can find."

"Okay."

"The interior vault. We need your code."

My code in fact opened a second vault door, into a smaller room where even more sensitive material was kept. That first day I mostly sat at the reading table while Brittany went over what she found, making notes, explaining it to me. I had a basic grasp of most of it, and some required explanation. I was carrying a B-average in business with a human resources concentration. This math shit was mostly there to be someone else's problem. Dad always used to say there was no better problem than someone else's problem. He also taught me to listen to my gut and trust my experts, let them do their jobs and reserve the high level decisions for myself.

"There's so much here," she said. "We can't finish today and I can't take any of this out of here."

"So, I come back. When?"

"Martin goes to meetings every Monday, so every Monday?"

"That works."

She looked up from the papers. "Maybe we could go over this tonight. Over dinner."

I sat up. "No. Miss Andrews, look, let's keep this strictly professional. I have a…" I almost said *fiancee*, "I have a girlfriend. That's not why I'm here."

"Oh. Sorry. I didn't mean," she brushed her hair back, "Um. Right. So…"

"See you Monday," I said. "If we're going to take that kind of time to keep doing this, I want you to keep an eye on what he's doing right now. Anything you can put together to prove he's dirty."

"I can do that."

"You have my cell number if you need anything. Don't hesitate to call for help. Be careful."

"I will."

"I should leave first. Let's not be seen together. Wait twenty minutes. You have a reason to be in here? If someone asks?"

"Yeah. We just ran into each other, that's all."

"Okay. I'll see you Monday. Don't email or text me anything, do it all in writing or by voice. I don't want somebody stumbling on what you're doing. I think we should go to the police now, but if I can't change your mind…"

"Not yet. I'm not ready. If I try and fail…"

I sighed. "Yeah, I read you. Fine, Monday."

I left first, as I suggested. I stopped in a few offices and said hello to some family friends, to make it look like I was there for a reason besides ducking into the vault for no readily apparent purpose.

When I got back to school, Eve was waiting for me. I copied a key to my room for her since we were living together in flagrant violation of the college rules. Not like I cared.

The key even said "Do Not Duplicate" on it. I'm a rebel.

"Where have you been?" she said, looking up from her book.

"Who, me? I was just out getting some air."

"It's five o'clock. Your last class ended at three."

I'd skipped class, but she didn't know that.

I answered her by scooping her up out of the chair. Eve was light as a feather then, and I was very strong. I picked her right up and kissed her, hard, and I could feel her worries melt away. There was a little jealous streak in my Eve. I thought it was endearing, really. Her father beat her down and ground her into dust but that iron core remained behind and she was bouncing back. She smiled, she laughed at my dumb jokes. Once that barrier was broken I found out how clever and subtle she was. I lifted her onto the bed and rolled on top of her. She slipped her legs around me and I felt the softness of her breasts through her sweat and smelled lilacs in her hair, and tasted her warm sweet lips for what felt like hours. Her stomach rumbled and she broke from a kiss, touching my shoulders.

"Let's eat, huh?"

We ended up ordering pizza out. I ordered a big bowl of boneless hot wings and split a double cheesy with Eve, a big cheese pizza with more cheese in the crust around the edge. She loved those, used to eat them backwards.

You know, it's the simple things. She wasn't looking at me when it hit me. She was chewing on a wad of mozzarella and dough and working on some complicated expected value problem, her blue eyes burning with concentration. The fading afternoon light made her hair glow, the way it did. I just stared at her for a while, and realized that Eve was the most wonderful thing that ever happened to me. I hated her father's guts but I couldn't hate him for bringing her to me. I should have done something sooner. I should have done something about the wedding. I should have found a way to protect Eve *and* protect my mother and protect all the people he was going to hurt in my name, prevent all the evil he was going to do.

The three worst words in the English language are *I should have*.

None of that mattered, now. I was going to shut Martin down, pull his hooks out of my birthright, and get him away from my mother. I was going to save the princess and live forever with her I my tower.

Dad would be proud.

She looked up from her meal and math. "What?"

"Nothing. I was just looking at you."

The next day I went to shop for engagement rings.

Chapter Sixteen

Victor

That damn ring burned a hole in my pocket. Figuratively, I mean.

It took me two weeks to pick out the right one. I decided to combine trips. It made a good excuse. Lots of jewelers in Philadelphia, most of them, as you would expect, on Jeweler's Row. It took three trips before I settled on the one I wanted. A big diamond in the middle, cut in a square shape, flanked by two sapphires on either side, and two more diamonds, all on a white gold band. The sapphires sparkled like her eyes. On the fourth trip into the city, I picked up the ring and carried it in my pocket while I was working with Brittany. That was the biggest mistake I ever made, I think.

If I'd gone to the police, if I'd used my head, but I didn't want to involve Eve until I knew it was lock tight, until I knew Martin would go down.

The detective work was boring as hell. After listening to an hour of Brittany explaining the intricacies of a IPO and what Martin was doing with this tire company was illegal, I was ready to stab out my own ear drums with an ice pick. I leaned on my hand and thought about the look on Eve's face when I took a knee before her. Dad told me I should never ask a girl until I already knew the answer. I was pretty confident Eve's answer would be yes. I fingered the ring box in my pocket and tried to decide when to ask the question, and how. Should I just do it, right then when I got back to the room? Take her out? Where? We ate at McDonalds once a week. Billionaires do not propose to their girlfriends at McDonalds. I should do something fancy, I decided, something memorable. It needed to be something important.

School was almost over. I'd do it at home, at the house. In the library, I think. I needed to talk to Mom, first.

"We have enough here to make a case," said Brittany, "what do we do?"

"Put it all together," I said. "Take some vacation. We'll set up a meeting. I think you need to meet Eve."

263

"Okay. It might be tough for me to sneak all this out. I think you should do it."

She never took her eyes off me.

"Yeah, good point. You'd be in a world of shit if you got caught walking out of here with this stuff." So would I, but that was beside the point. Or maybe it was the point.

Victor, you asshole, you picked this day to be chivalrous.

I put the files in my attache. It was actually my father's, a hand me down from *his* father, old and supple and soft. I used to play with it when I was a kid, and beg my father to let me have it. Then when it was mine, I didn't want it anymore. I didn't want any of this. I just wanted to work on cars.

Get rid of Martin and I could.

I left first, as we usually did. No one searched me, of course, as I left.

Graduation was the following week. I would walk, get my diploma, and step onto the football field one of the one hundred richest men in the world. All my dreams were coming true. I never dreamed about the money. Honestly, I wasn't even sure what to do with it. Materially, I already had everything I could possibly want or need, and soon Eve would, too, and our kids. I wanted kids with her, I was one hundred and ten percent sure, and she was coming around. She would finish her degree. We'd live off campus for her last year. I was already looking at houses. I was going to surprise her with it. We both liked the town, and I was thinking maybe we'd move there. I could shutter the house, turn it into a museum, maybe we could winter there or something. It was a long drive back. I had a lot of time, a lot of dreaming to do.

Technically, we could have lived in the dorm until my graduation, but I packed all of mine and Eve's shit in the back of the car, filling up the trunk and seat both, and we drove home. The only thing missing was a just married sign and some cans to rattle behind us as we drove. I was giddy with excitement. I'd already talked to the kitchen staff. We were going to eat on the terrace, have a big fancy meal and then I'd pop the question at sunset, drop to one knee before her and wait for her to answer. The idea made my palms sweat. When I was shopping for the ring I was sure she'd say yes. Now that she was sitting next to me, sleeping with head propped on my shoulder as I drove the back way up the country roads, I wasn't so sure. It was a silly kind of worry, like checking the stove three times before leaving the house, or running around looking for your keys when they're in your hand.

Reminds me of something my Dad told me once. Love is giving someone the power to hurt you terribly, and hoping they don't.

I didn't wake her until we were almost home. I nudged her with my arm and she stirred, yawned, and stretched, folding her arms behind her head and cracking her back.

"Hey," I said. "We're back."

She looked a little sad, but then she always did.

"I'm going to talk to my mother," I said.

She looked at me sharply, drawing in a quick breath.

"Eve, in a week it won't matter what anybody says. We can do what we want."

She nodded. "What about... I mean, legally. I never looked it up. I was afraid."

"What, because our parents are married? It means nothing legally, Eve. I talked to a company lawyer about it. People might think it's weird or tacky, but fuck them. I do what I want."

She always flinched when I used a curse word casually like that.

"My father…"

"Can go fuck himself. We're adults, Eve, and there's nothing he can do. If he tries, my lawyers will blot out the sun."

Besides, there would be no need to worry about him, soon. Maybe she'd want to visit him in prison.

Eve settled into her seat as I pulled around to the garage. I wanted to carry my own stuff but Mom insisted the servants do it. I never liked having *servants*. It felt so silly, to have people paid to carry my crap. Eve felt the same way, but we went along with it.

Mom looked healthier than she had for a while. She picked up a bad cough over the winter and lingered for months, all through the rest of the school year. She'd been pale and drawn, but looked bright and healthy today. She gave me a big hug, then gave one to Eve, squeezing the life out of her.

"My father?" said Eve.

"Away on business," she sighed. "He's been so distant lately, I..." she looked at Eve. "Nevermind about that. Come in. I haven't seen either of you since Easter."

It took an hour of talking to pry her away from Eve. We went to Dad's old study. I thought it was the best place.

When she hacked and coughed into her hand, it worried me. She was carrying around a hanky to cough into.

"Hey," I said. "Have you been to the doctor about that?"

"It's nothing. So what's the big secret?"

I leaned back on his desk and fiddled with his magnifying glass. "Eve and I have, um," I started. How do I put this?

"You're in a relationship, Vic. I'm not blind. Did you really think anyone bought your excuses to get away from here with her? I'm not that slow."

She smiled warmly at me.

"Yeah. I"m going to ask her to marry me. Tonight."

"Good. I hope she says yes. She loves you, you know."

I thought I was going to fall through the floor. "Yeah. Thanks, Mom."

"Of course. Martin isn't going to like this."

My face must have hardened, because she raised her hand.

"You know, you were right. Marrying him was a mistake."

My hands tightened around the edge of the desk and the wood dug into my palms. "Why? Did he-"

"Hit me? No. He just grew less and less interested in me as the years went on. It's been, what, three years now? The closer we came to the day the trust passed to you, the less interested in me he became."

Another coughed wracked her tiny body, and I felt my stomach sink. Maybe it was just the lighting in the office, but Mom looked *old*. She'd never looked *old*. Not like that. She swept at her lips with the hanky and tucked it into her pocket, and folded her arms.

"What are you going to do?"

"I don't know. What should I do? I've been thinking about a separation."

"There's stuff I haven't told you about him. About the way he raised his daughter."

"I knew there was something strange about it," she sighed. "The homeschooling was... odd. It almost sounds like he had her locked up, isolated from the outside world, doesn't it? I thought he was just overprotective. He can be very intense."

"He used to hit her. Badly. He left scars, Mom."

Startled, she blinked. "He never raised a hand against me. Why haven't you said this before?"

I wasn't sure I could be rid of him before.

"I talked to him once, made sure it wouldn't be a problem with you, or with Eve anymore. Did he tell you he came to our school the first year she was there and tried to kidnap her? He was going to force her to transfer because I transferred there to join her."

Another sigh. It turned into a fit of coughing again.

I could have sworn I saw a spot of red on the handkerchief.

"It's nothing," she said, before I could ask. "Just a damned cough, it'll go away."

It worried me, but lots of things worried me. I had the ring in my pocket. I was giddy with excitement, more alive than I'd felt in years. I never thought I could possibly be this *happy*. Mom hugged me.

"I hope everything goes as you have planned. Go get yourself cleaned up and get ready. You've had a long drive. I'll keep Eve busy until it's time for you to eat."

Gleefully, I rushed to my room and cleaned myself up. I'd arranged to eat at dusk, giving me plenty of time to relax. The sun would set after eight tonight. Eve, I knew, was getting settle in herself, and would want some time alone.

Sleep came easier than I thought, but it was fitful and harsh and I spent the whole time tossing and turning, waking every hour or so to check the clock. When it was finally time, I dressed. Nothing fancy, just clothes. Eve was already outside. Somebody lit a pair of taper candles on the table on the terrace, the one where Mom and Martin ate lunch with Eve the day I first set eyes on her. Dinner was nothing fancy, either. Grilled chicken and rice. We ate quietly, enjoying each other's company and the warm air. The breeze behind the house always smelled like the woods, deep and earthy and ancient, but when it picked up just the right way I could smell the lilacs. Eve. When she finished her portion her silverware clinked softly on her plate.

"Desert?" I said.

"Yeah."

"I have something to ask you first."

Here we go.

I got up and walked to her side, and dropped to one knee. A grin spread on her face and that was all the answer I needed. I took the ring in its little box from my pocket.

Then the spotlight hit me, blinded me, and Eve screamed.

The world went crazy. It sounded like thunder, *whup whup whup*, but it was the blade of a helicopter. The blasting wind blew out the candles, and knocked them over, and sent napkins flying from the table. I fell back on my ass, covering my eyes as Eve kept screaming, covering hers with both arms. All of a sudden men in black were everywhere, and they had guns. I started to get up but there was a knee in my back and all of a sudden two hundred plus pounds was pushing down into the middle of my spine and someone was yanking my wrists back. I thought they were going to break my arms. Mom came running out of the house, screaming at them. One of the black-clad men grabbed her arm and she went down hard on the terrace, and I saw blood on her lips and bellowed in fury, trying to buck loose, almost tearing my own shoulders out of joint as they cuffed me.

It was only then that someone barked, *"Federal Bureau of Investigation!"*

I went still.

What? What the absolute *fuck?*

There was a gun pressed to the back of my head.

"Stop moving."

I looked around. Jesus, there had to be fifty of them on the lawn. Where did they all come from?

Hysterical, I looked around. I dropped the damn ring. It was sitting on the stone floor of the terrace.

Eve picked it up, and opened, and looked at me.

"I don't know what this is about," I shouted, "I'll take care of it. Go inside with Mom."

"Shut up," the FBI man barked.

They pulled me up by the arms, painfully. They dragged me through the house, where they were ransacking everything. There was a van waiting out front, one of a dozen black vehicles. They dragged me inside and sat between two guys with rifles dressed up like ninjas, like I was going to do something terrible if they didn't watch me every second. It was only then that a man in a suit stepped into the van and the doors slapped closed behind him. He was the stereotypical G-man, right down to the mirrored aviators and the chewing gum. He chewed loudly, stared me down. I stared right back. I didn't know what this was about, but whatever it was I was innocent, I'd done nothing wrong and I was absolutely certain I could prove it.

"Victor Amsel," he said, "You have the right to remain silent."

He ran through all the rights. You know how it goes.

I chose to exercise my right to remain silent, but not before I snarled, "Fuck you, asshole."

That seemed to amuse him. He sat back.

"You're a big fish," he said, staring me down. "Make my career."

I said nothing. I knew at least that much. I wasn't going to talk my way out of this, and the more I talked the more I'd mouth off and give them something to use against me. I'd find out what I was charged with later. Mom would be calling the lawyers now. We had people on retainer. I'd be out by morning.

I kept telling myself, I'd be out by morning.

As they booked me, I'd be out by morning.

As they fingerprinted me, I'd be out by morning.

As they took mug shots, I'd be out by morning.

As they took my clothes and made me put on an orange jumpsuit, I'd be out by morning.

As they locked me in a solitary holding cell on the four floor of the grim block of a jail house, I'd be out by morning.

By early afternoon the next day, I stopped lying to myself. I waited for the visit, for Eve and Mom to show up and tell me it was going to be alright, this was all a huge mistake, this would be taken care of and I'd take my graduation walk and get my birthright and marry the girl of my dreams. This was all just a temporary pit stop on the road to happily ever after.

Neither Mom, nor Eve, came to see me.

A federal prosecutor did.

They took me to an interrogation room. Later I learned they called it *the fish tank*. It was a square, ugly room of unadorned concrete with a steel table. In the middle was a ring, bolted to the metal. They put a pair of those long shackles on my wrists with the chain running through the loop on the table, so I couldn't get away.

I named him Junior G-Man in my head.

"Ronald Powers," he introduced himself.

"Go fuck yourself," I replied, cheerily.

"That's not a very good way to start our conversation."

276

"You're not here to help me. I'm not going to get out of this by talking to you. I have nothing to say."

He sat down and made a cutting motion across his neck with his hand. I flinched, until I realized he was signaling someone on the other side of the bulletproof glass.

It meant *stop recording*.

That made me a little nervous.

"Off the record. Not so brave now, are you, you little prick?"

"What do you want?"

"When the mikes come back on, which has to be fast because we're going to say it's a technical error, we're going to negotiate a plea deal."

"I'm not talking to you without my lawyer."

"Shut up and listen. You take the conviction. Plead out. We'll give you a light sentence. Two years."

Two years of my life for something I didn't even do? I was about tell him what I thought about that, and him, and his ugly necktie, when he raised his hand.

"I know it's a shitty deal. Here's the other condition."

He dropped a folder on the table. My chains rattled as I pulled it to me and spread it open.

Pictures of me and Brittany. At the pizza parlor. Surveillance stills of me walking into the vault after she did.

So what? Were they threatening her, or...

Oh.

Oh *God*.

"We show the girl the pictures. Proof you've been fucking another woman."

"I didn't," I snap. "I never, this is a lie-"

"That's not you?"

"It is. I was working with her to gather evidence on..." I trailed off.

"Working with her missionary, or bent over the desk?"

"Asshole," I snarled. "Fuck you. I'm not taking any deal. You don't have shit on me, I didn't do anything illegal. So go fuck yourself."

He made a gesture. The tapes were rolling again. I couldn't tell, exactly, I could just feel it.

Christ.

"So," he said, "Let's talk deal."

"Lawyer," I said.

Four hours of pleading, yelling, threatening, arguing, reasoning, and then finally stony silence, and I never said another word.

I was one hundred percent certain that Eve would take my side, that she would never, ever believe a filthy lie about me cheating on her.

I didn't figure on one thing.

I didn't figure on Brittany backing up their bullshit.

Chapter Seventeen

Victor

It was a long six weeks in that solitary cell. Technically, it was a luxury, to protect the rich boy from general population. I was in jail, not yet in prison, where they house petty criminals serving short sentences along with people who've been arrested and charged but not yet tried, or are undergoing trial. Still, there were plenty of people there that would get off on teaching the rich boy a lesson. They let me out to eat lunch, at least, and I got an hour of exercise a day.

I spent that pacing in circles in a caged-in pen, by myself, watched by a guard who looked about as interested in me as I was in the cracks on the floor, which depending on the day could be not at all or very intensely. I had my lawyer in the first twenty-four hours. He was a friend of my Dad's, a good guy named Morty Grieg. He brought with him a partner, a woman named Claire Barnes. Together, they promised me they would take care of all of this.

They didn't.

The trial lasted for seventeen days. That translated to three weeks, since we skipped a Wednesday because a juror had a doctor's appointment and the trial did not continue on Fridays. Everything was very stiff and formal. This was federal court, I was charged with federal crimes. Insider trading, wire fraud, and embezzlement.

The biggest piece of evidence was the papers in my attache, and all the papers in the vault with my fingerprints on them. Brittany wasn't watching Martin, she was setting me up. She showed me paper after paper, even had me sign stuff, and I didn't realize what I was doing. The vault recorded every time I was in and out and there were signatures from the sign-in books, and they brought in people to testify that I'd been seen more frequently in the office for the last six weeks or so. I just sat there and absorbed it. My lawyers would tear them apart. It didn't mean jack shit, there was no proof I actually did anything, only that I knew. I was waiting for the big Perry Mason moment when my lawyers would turn and dramatically accuse Martin where he sat in the gallery with Mom and Eve.

Any comfort that thought might bring me turned to ashes in my mouth when I saw her. Eve looked like somebody died. Her eyes were always red, and there were tracks burned in her cheeks from crying. She looked like a drowned rat in ill fitting clothes, staring down at the floor most of the time with my mother's arm around her, listening.

They had other evidence. It was all bullshit but they had it.

They spun a story and it went like this: Some three years ago when I started sleeping with Martin's daughter, I began scheming to get rid of him, because he could catch me at my games. According to the prosecution, I'd been running the company behind the scenes for two full years while Martin was in the dark, trying to put out my fires without knowing the cause. His main concern was maintaining the trust and my family's accounts, and his wife.

I wanted to throw up.

My instrument to achieve this was Brittany. She lied to me, she hadn't been working with the company for a few weeks, she'd been working at

Amsel since she graduated from college herself, almost four years ago.

According to them, it was two years ago when we started the affair.

Immunity. They gave her *immunity* to testify against me.

The rest of it was a blur, but I remember the day she said her piece with crystalline, focused clarity.

She sat in the witness box in a dark suit, like she was going to a funeral. Her frizzy hair was smoothed, bound in a severe bun. She looked twice as old as she did the day I met her, but she had a childlike vulnerability that must have absolutely wowed the jury. She sat primly in the box and waited.

Ronald Powers asked the questions himself.

"Can you tell us your full name?"

"Brittany Lynne Andrews."

They had her swear in. No book or So Help Me God like TV, it was all very formal.

When she was done with that he looked over at me and said, "Can you identify that man, please."

"His name is Victor Amsel."

"Thank you. Can you describe the nature of your relationship with him?"

She cleared her throat, and turned red. It was very, very convincing. I would have been fooled myself. She looked guiltily at the jury, looked past me at Eve, and never once set her eyes on me. She swallowed hard and said, "For the last two years, he and I were engaged in a sexual affair."

You could hear a pin drop, except for the soft sound of weeping. Eve.

I didn't look at her. I couldn't make myself.

Stop it, I thought. I was starting to get angry with her. How *dare* she believe this bullshit. My hands clenched into fists.

Morty grabbed my arm. "Quiet," he murmured.

"That's not at issue here," Powers said, slyly. "What else can you tell us about your relationship?"

"It is an issue," she said, calmly. "That's how it started. I didn't know he had a girlfriend. I'm older, dedicated to my career. I didn't get out much, and the heir to the company was showering me with attention, but he was just using me."

"How was he using you?"

She sniffed and scrubbed at her eyes. "He needed me to cover his tracks. He's been stealing money from the company and running bust-outs on some of the companies Amsel bought into for over two years now. I kept notes."

"You did?"

"I did. I thought… I thought he was going to… propose to me," she said, sighing. "He bought an engagement ring. He took me with him to look at it, but it was for *her*. Then he came to me with this plan. He was going to blow everything open and blame his stepfather. He needed to get rid of him. Everything we did was a constant game of cat and mouse, avoiding Martin Ross catching us in the act. I was terrified. When I wanted to stop, he threatened me."

"Threatened you?"

"Yes. He said I was nothing to someone like him, he could make me disappear with a phone call and no one would care. I was scared, so I started putting together a file. Like insurance. I started getting material to tie him to his crimes. Then I found out he was going to propose to Martin's daughter. He… he *hit me*," she broke down, "he said if I told anyone about us he'd kill me himself, and-"

"Objection," Morty snarled, "This is all hearsay, and-"

"Overruled," the judge said, calmly.

I blinked. It wasn't supposed to work like that. I mean, the whole objection-overruled thing is a TV schtick, right? They usually go talk in the judge's office and shit. What the hell was this? Morty was purple, beside himself with fury. His partner leaned over and whispered.

"Let them. This is all fodder for the appeal. They don't have anything on you, Vic. They have no evidence. What they do have points to Martin!"

There was a commotion behind me. Mom and Martin led Eve out of the gallery. She was sobbing, her shoulders shaking. She was completely breaking down and there was nothing I could do. I was chained to the fucking floor. The bailiff gave me the stink eye if I even thought about getting up, like he just *knew*.

The rest of Brittany's testimony was boring. Dates and places we met, half of them fabricated.

It went on for almost five hours. There was a lot of information.

That evening, I was led out of the holding cell. Morty and Claire were waiting for me in the fish tank, with Powers. The guards sat me down, chained me to the table, and stepped out.

"We're here for a plea bargain," Morty said to me, his voice heavy with doubt.

"This is what happens," said Powers, seating himself across from me. "You had your shot, rich boy. You sign the papers now and take this plea agreement. If you do not, tomorrow we will call Evelyn Ross to the stand and ask her several very pointed questions.

"About what?"

"Where you were, what you were doing, and where you told *her* you were on several key dates."

"This is bullshit," Claire declared, firmly. "Don't take anything, don't sign anything, Vic."

"How long?" I rasped.

"Six years. Five with good behavior."

"Their case is a joke," Morty said to me. "This is a formality. Don't take the deal."

"If I don't take it, you call Eve to testify," I said.

"That's right," Powers said, softly. "What do you think about that?"

"Six years. Five with good behavior."

I slid the papers over to Morty. "Read this and make sure he's not lying about what it says."

"Vic…" Claire said, pleading with me.

"Just do it."

Morty gave me a sad look. "For the sake of the love I bore your father, don't sign this."

"Is it legit?"

"Yea. You'll be pleading to lesser chargers, they agreed to drop a couple."

"It doesn't matter. I could go to jail for a week and I still lose my inheritance."

"Prison," Powers corrected. "Jail is for pre-trial detention. Your inheritance. Oh no, we couldn't have you lose that."

"I don't give a fuck about my inheritance. Just leave Evelyn alone."

I signed the papers. I signed my life away.

I couldn't let them put Eve up there. I had to find another way. I just needed to talk to her.

Things proceeded. Eve did not attend the trial after that. It wasn't much of one. The judge read over the agreement, approved it. Words were said. I was remanded to custody.

I went to prison.

First thing, it wasn't like the movies. There wasn't a whole thing with a bunch of guys shouting fresh fish, nor was I going to a hardcore supermax. In fact, I was going to medium security, one step above let-you-out-on weekends. They were not letting me out on weekends. I had to go through the whole procedure again, get a new uniform, still bright orange.

It was pretty late when they led me into my cell and I met my cellmate. I didn't know what to expect. He was on the bottom bunk, reading a book propped open in the biggest, hairiest hands I've ever seen. Every part of him was hairy except for his shiny bald egg head. I thought he was fat at first but he was all mass, moving with a strange grace when I walked into the cell carrying an armful of cheap, stiff linens. My mattress looked more like a blanket. It didn't matter. It could be a king-size memory foam whatever and it would be the worst bed in the world without Eve. It was starting to sink in that it was all over, that I would never be waking up next to her again. I must have just stood there for a while.

"Vitali," my cellmate announced, thrusting out his hand.

I dropped my things on the top bunk and took his hand. He gave me a firm, almost brutal shake.

"Victor."

"I know who you are. I have pulled strings to make sure you are bunked here. You are Victor Amsel. They call me Vitali the Hammer."

Oh shit. *That* Vitali.

"What are you doing here?"

I probably shouldn't have shown fear, but at that moment I was scared shitless. This was the Vitali that Brittany was always talking about, the one I was supposed to be setting up to take a fall along with Martin.

"You are afraid I am going to kill you."

I blinked a few times. "Yeah."

"I would not kill you. I would have someone else kill you. I am not wanting to go to supermax." His Russian accent started poking out, rounding out his vowels, making him sound a little harsh. "No. I bring you here because I am wanting to be your friend."

"I've been told not to make friends here," I said.

Actually, no one told me that. I saw it in a movie. Also, it made a hell of a lot of sense. Vitali was not the kind of guy I wanted on my speed dial.

"Five years will be a long time," he said, folding his hands between his legs. "I have been here for two already, and I am looking at six more. I am behaving but they will be strict with me."

"I see," I said. "Well, good luck with that."

I climbed up on that top bunk.

"If you will not let me help you, I will have to use you."

I froze, sitting there. There wasn't much room. My head brushed the ceiling and I flopped down.

"Use me how?"

"You will help me destroy Martin. You can do this and gain from it, or you can be forced."

"I'm not doing anything that's going to keep me in here longer, and I don't want to have any trouble with you, but I'm not going to put myself in your debt either."

He sighed. "You should hear me out. You wouldn't want this Eve to have an accident, would you?"

I sat up. "What?"

I also hit my head on the ceiling, and went crashing back down. Fuck. I was out of the bunk and on my feet in seconds, seeing red. I didn't care if I spent the rest of my life in this shithole, nobody was going to use Eve against me. Nobody was going to threaten her.

Vitali sat up.

"You are hotheaded. I was like this in my youth."

"Listen, fuckhead. You put one hand on Eve and I'll fucking kill you. You have to sleep sometime."

"I won't put a hand on her. Friends of mine will do that, and more. After what Martin did to me, I should feed him her liver, but I don't think he would care. Martin is not like other men. He does not *feel*. I would be more frightened of him in this room than all your youthful bluster. In any case, if you threaten me again, Eve will suffer the consequences. Now sit down and we will talk."

There was no where to sit, besides his bunk, but the toilet. I sat on the toilet and propped my cheek on my chin.

"Good. Now you are listening, I am speaking. I have plan to deal with Martin and return to you what is yours, minus some, shall we say, recompense for my situation. Two years ago, Martin betrayed me to police. Arranged that I would be caught red handed."

"He's been sending you money, though," I said. "To a bunch of fake Russian companies…"

"All his, created with me. When he decided he no longer had use of my services, he disposed of me. I think I should consider myself lucky. If our situations were reversed, I would have had him killed." Vitali shrugged.

The causal way he said it made me shudder.

"This is agreement. You work for me, help me undo Martin. I leave girl alone, cut you in."

"Define 'cut me in'. I don't want to be looking over my shoulder for the rest of my life."

"No, no, bad for business. I only torture and kill men who screw me over. Fulfill your end of the agreement and it is done when it is done, no more between us. Yes?"

I looked around. With my luck, this was another setup.

"You refuse, Eve has trouble."

"Fine, fine, god damn it," I snapped. "What do I have to do?"

"Wait," said Vitali. "For five long years, wait, learn, and prepare. Then Martin will wish he had never been born."

Wait I did. I waited, and waited, and waited.

After the end of the first month, I thought I was going crazy. That was when Mom came to visit me. The only time she came to visit me. I sat in the visiting room, my leg jagging up and down as I scrubbed my hands through my hair. It wasn't like the movies, with the glass partition and the phone. It was just a table in a room, though I was shackled to the floor by the ankles. I sat there wringing my hands for an hour, forgot the shackles, and tried to stand up when she came in.

She looked *bad*. She must have lost twenty pounds, she was pale, her skin was waxy. She walked over to the table and sat down and stared at me flatly.

"How could you?"

"*Mom?*" I choked out. "You can't believe this. I didn't do anything."

She shook her head. "Victor, it was all going to be yours. Why did you do this?" She snorted. "I should have known. I'd hoped you were just going through a phase, with all those girls. When you started seeing Eve I really thought you loved her. You were sleeping with that slut almost the whole time, weren't you?"

"No. *No*, Mom, I swear."

"They showed us pictures. Pictures of you eating with her. Holding hands."

"For Christ's sake, Mom," I pleaded, "she touched my hand. I pulled away..."

It hit me then like a ton of bricks. It was *all* a setup, the whole fucking routine. She touched my hand for the benefit of the photographer they had following me.

Martin saw the end was near. He had to know I'd have him out of there the instant I had legal control of the company. How many favors did he call in? I never had a chance. My lawyers could have called Jesus Christ to the witness stand to testify in my defense and the jury would still have convicted me. I just spared Eve some suffering by keeping her off the stand. The result would have been the same. How long had he been planning this? Since that day he tried to drive her away? Before she started college?

Since I met her? Was this the plan the whole time, drive a wedge into my family?

Holy God, if I couldn't inherit, which I now could not, the entire estate reverted to my mother.

Who had, no doubt, made Eve her sole beneficiary. She was like a daughter to her.

"Mom?" I said, softly. "What's wrong?'

"I had to see you again. I'm dying, Victor. I have lung cancer."

I blurted out, "but you don't *smoke.*"

She started laughing, and stopped herself when it turned into a wet, thick cough. "I know. It's hilarious. First I lose my husband, and now this. Eve is devastated, Victor. She cries day and night. She missed her final exams. She thought you loved her."

"I do, I do I swear. I signed a plea deal so she wouldn't have to testify. I'd do anything. Please tell her, Mom. I love her. Look at me. *Look at me.*"

She looked at me. From her eyes, you'd think she was dead already.

There was a sliver of doubt there, though. Just a touch.

No matter what, she was still my Mom.

"I might tell her, when she calms down and can think rationally. She really does love you, Victor. I don't know what it's going to do to her, going through this."

She stood up. Time was up.

Before she left she said, "Wait. I do know. It's going to make her like *him.*"

She coughed again.

"Mom," I said. "I love you."

She walked out. They closed the door.

Five years is a long time.

Chapter Eighteen

Evelyn

Neither of us speaks for a long time.

Finally, I clear my throat, and fill the air. "You claim it was all a setup," I say, softly.

Victor looks at me. His face is hard but his eyes, his eyes are pleading.

"It was. I swear to God, they made it all up. It was a trick. I never thought they would try to make it look like I was sleeping with Brittany."

"You weren't sleeping with her," I say.

"No. I swear it on my mother's grave. I was not sleeping with Brittany Andrews. Or anybody else after I met you. Not since the *day* I met you. I even had some girl pawing at me at our parents' wedding."

"I remember that, you blew her off."

"I would again, and again, every time for a thousand years for you, Eve. I love you."

The words hit me like hammers. I. Love. You.

I want to say it back, but if it was true I wouldn't have believed the lies, would I?

"You took the conviction to spare me?"

He looks up at me and nods, slowly. "Yeah. I knew it would be brutal for you if they put you on the stand, and I knew there was nothing I could do to stop it. My lawyers couldn't even stop it. The whole thing was crooked. Your father had control of the money, and money buys power."

I shake my head. He stands up and walks over to the bed. I hug my knees to my chest and curl up, waiting. He sits down. I look over through the fringe of my hair as he sits on the bed and, gingerly, reaches out and touches my back.

My voice comes out tiny, childlike. I can't help it.

"A-after that your Mom got really bad," I blurt out. "She got sick very fast. It was weeks. She spent the last two months in the hospital. I visited her every day even when I was supposed to be studying. Father pulled strings and got my degree conferred on me on time. He moved all of your stuff out of your room."

He tugs on the hood of my sweatshirt.

"You kept this."

I nod, and sniff back tears. "I used to sleep in it. I hid it from him so he wouldn't know. I kept the ring, too. I still have it."

He reaches over and touches my chin with his fingers. A little tug and I turn to face him, still curled up. He looks right into my eyes.

"Evelyn Ross, I swear, I did not sleep with anyone but you. I didn't do anything they accused me of. I saw proof that your father is a criminal."

My mouth works silently, but I can't say anything.

Finally, I manage to choke it out. "I'm sorry."

"Why didn't you see me?"

"I couldn't," I whisper, "at first. After that... Father was always there. When your mother died, I was alone with him. I started to *forget*. It went back to the way it was. I was alone with him in the house all the time. It was like he knew what I was thinking. Then I just..."

I take a long breath.

"It hurt so much, I just didn't want to feel *anything*. When I lost your mother, I was crushed. There was nothing left. I was like a robot. I woke up, went to work, slept, woke up, went to work. The only time I felt something was when people were afraid of me. It made me feel strong. Like I meant something."

Victor puts his arms around me. I stay still at first. Part of me is still fighting it, but it hurts too much and I don't have the strength anymore. I give in. I collapse against him, but I don't cry. My eyes are dry. I just press them shut. Then they start to sting a little and I feel an itch on my cheeks and lie to myself, and almost believe it's not tears. Then the sobbing starts and I slip my arms around Vic's broad chest and squeeze him, hard. He breathes against me, sitting still at first, and slowly puts his arms around me.

"We used to be really good," he says.

"I'm sorry," I mumble, over and over. "I'm so sorry. I should have carried her message."

"What did she say?"

"She was in the hospital. Near the end. She told me that she forgave you that I needed to forgive you, that if I went and saw you and gave you a chance I'd understand, but then she was gone and I was alone with *him*. He *hit me*, Victor. After the meeting he was there when I got home and he *hit me*."

I break down in sobs. Victor is still as stone, but his embrace is warm and firm. Slowly, he lays down, pulling me with him so I'm curled up to his side and tucked up under his arm. He reaches over and grabs a fistful of the dry, scratchy hotel room tissues and dabs the tears from my face.

"You're melting," he says.

I snort. "I hate that fucking article. Ice Queen? Really?"

"I think it's cute. You do look like some sort of ice fairy princess."

I laugh softly. Can it be this easy?

"What kind of a deal did you make? Are you in trouble?"

"Yeah," he says, softly, "I'm in trouble. I'll probably never be safe. I did it for you."

"Don't throw that at me," I say, bitterly. "I can't take that, too. God, Victor, what was wrong with me? I shouldn't have believed…"

He cuts me off and squeezes my arm. "Eve, I think if I was in the gallery *I* would have believed it. They played me hard, like a sucker. I should have known when she propositioned me. Twice. Fucking bitch."

He sits up and leaves me lying on the bed. I run my hands up his back.

"What do we do?"

"I don't know. I can't stop what I'm doing now. I work for Vitali. You know why the call him the hammer? He told me when you smash a guy's toes with a hammer, they look like grapes. Jesus."

"What exactly is it you're supposed to do?"

"Run a bust out on Amsel. Destroy my own company. I get a cut of the proceeds. He keeps the rest. If the company was public I could move on it when the stock price goes down, but it's still privately held. I was going to try and force Martin to take the company public, spread out the debts before it came down on him. On you."

"Can I give it to you?"

"What?"

I sit up next to him. "I know when you were convicted, you were automatically disinherited. Then it passed to your mother, then when she died, to me, per her will. Some of your distant relatives tried to sue but it went nowhere."

He sighed. "I don't care about the company, or the money. I want you, Eve. I want you by my side."

I squeeze his hand.

"What do we do?"

He squeezes back. "You go back to work. We start working together to put your father away."

I tense, and suck in a sharp breath. "Victor, I can't. He'll know, he…"

"He won't. We have to play pretend. You have to make him think you still hate me. I have a plan of my own. Do you trust me?"

"Yes," I whisper.

"Good. We'll talk about this later. Does your father know where you are?"

"No."

"Would he have any reason to look here?"

"No."

"Good," he says.

He turns, quick and lithe, and his arms are around me, all at once, then his lips on mine as he pushes me down into the bed. I slide my arms around his neck and my legs spread around his sides. It's been so long, I'm aching for it. He kisses me hungrily, aggressively, like he doesn't want to stop but he can't wait any longer to attack my throat. It's cold in the room but I don't care. His hands are cold on my skin when the slip up under my sweatshirt. He unhooks my bra as deftly as he always did, like it was yesterday the last time we did this. Once it's loose I'm shedding my clothes, t-shirt and hoodie and underwear and loose pants, and tugging the sheets down. Victor looks at me body like he's never seen me before. He looks at me like he's never seen a woman before. I pull on his shirt. It's only fair.

He peels off the damp t-shirt, stands up and gets out of his jeans, yanks off his socks. He's rock hard and just as big as I remember. Victor dives into the bed, skimming lightly over me as he kisses me again. The heater blasts warm air into the room, but I shiver at every touch, at his lips on my throat, his hands on my breasts, the feel of his erection pressed against my stomach. I want him inside me now. I want to feel again. He cradles my head in my hands and kisses me forever, until it burns. The heat between my thighs is a furnace. I writhe under him, naked and wanting, urge him on but he refuses to indulge me, instead tortures me by savoring me. His lips on my throat now, his hands moving slowly down my sides, turning each beat of my heart into a drum beat, faster, faster, faster, *now*, but it's not now, I have to wait.

Victor honestly enjoys going down on me, I think. He does it whenever he can. His touch is hesitant. I only feel his breath at first, then it's like he remembers. His hands slide under my butt and squeeze and my stomach flexes as I angle my hips, and press my legs around his head and pull him in, one hand knotted in his hair. Then his mouth, hot on my skin, working up the inside of my thigh to my throbbing sex. Suddenly I was happy he was taking his time. I spent so long trying to please myself with my own hands, imagining Victor down there, and now he's real again. I know he's real because I feel the heat of his breath, the warm wet touch of his tongue, and I hear the little noise he makes when he tastes me, so much like hunger. I look down and see the lust in his eyes and heat spread through my chest, like a deep breath of hot air. I need this so badly it hurts. I feel alive again. Please, please, please.

He takes his time, slowly at first, teasing my lips, before his finger slowly enters me. I hear him gasp, see the slack expression on his face before it turns to a grin and he looks up before dipping down to suck lightly on my clit, and I groan and writhe on the bed. The heater is running too hard, it's too hot in here. I'm sweating all over, between my shoulder blades, my chest, my forehead, under my arms. The heat grows with every touch, and every passing moment. I need more. As my arousal builds, so does his. I can feel it radiating off him, like heat. My body quivers around his finger, a shock of pleasure jolts down my legs and I curl up, biting down a little sound. Slowly, Victor rises, drawing his finger from my body. He rubs it on my lips and I taste myself on his skin, suck his finger. He lowers himself on top of me.

"You want me to eat you out until you cum," he whispers in my ear, "Or fuck you silly?"

My answer is a light tug on his cock with my fingers. It feels so good to touch him again, to feel his response. As he slides into me I watch the muscles of his back ripple. It's a full body motion, his rod plunging into my wet sex, spreading my quivering walls, filling me. I groan and splay out on the bed, lazily holding him around the neck as he begins to thrust into me. He's urgent at first, each pump building the pleasure, the fullness growing with each stroke, bigger, bigger, more, more, but then he slows, like he remembers how long it's been and decides to savor me. When he slowly draws almost all the way out of me and slowly presses back in, shuddering with forced restraint, the pleasure is so intense it nearly hurts and I whimper and shudder under him, my muscles tensing with every jerk and shock of sensation that rolls through my body.

Then he settles on top of me and kisses me hard and deep, and I take him deep, his rod shifting inside me as he remains buried and rolls his hips. He rests his weight on me, buries his face in my neck, and his whole body trembles with anticipation. I rake my nails down his back, heat pulsing through me in slow throbs, spreading from between my legs to radiate down to my toes, down to my fingertips, swirl under my scalp. I'm sliding away on a tide of pleasure. My legs wrap around him and I pull him against me and a second dragging scratch on his back sends him into a sudden burst of energy, fucking me hard and fast. I need it so bad. I clench around him, all my muscles going tight as taut wires. I whimper and plead in his ear, now, now, *please*, I want his pleasure as much as I want mine, just the idea of it will make me explode. If I go one more day frozen in ice, I'll die.

Victor drives deep into me, pins me to the bed, and grunts in my ear. The grunts turn into a low, throaty moan, louder than he means it to be, breathy, then louder again as I feel him throbbing, finishing, and explode, thrashing under him. It feel so good the pleasure edges nearly into pain, and I dig my nails into his back and *bite him*, quiet now as pleasure wracks my body in shuddering, punishing waves. When it finally ends I go limp under him, spread out on the bed. He looks at the mark on his shoulder from my teeth and kisses me, hard. I feel wet on his back. I drew blood with my nails. He lays on top of me, *in me*, and doesn't pull away.

This is being home. I'm home.

God, how could I ever have doubted him.

"Mine," I purr into his throat. "Mine."

Eventually, he pulls out of me and I scoot back on the bed to lay plastered to his side, wrapped in his arm. He breathes under me, his chest rising and falling in huge, muscular rhythm. He falls asleep and I could sleep with him like this, forever. I trace my fingers over the designs on his skin. Sometimes he stirs in his sleep, holds me a little tighter, then goes limp again as he falls deeper into sleep once more. By the time he wakes up again I think I've traced every feather incised on his skin twice. His eyes open and he looks at me and without a word, I slip down between his legs, my slick sweaty skin gliding over his, and take his cock in my mouth. I close my eyes and rest my head on his leg and let him harden slowly between my lips, tasting myself on his shaft. It doesn't take long. A few flicks of my tongue and he stiffens again, groaning.

I take my time. He's already cum inside me, so he lasts longer. The way he grunts and paws the sheets and tugs at my hair when I'm sucking him off makes me feel feral, sexual. I remember the first time I did this, I felt submissive, even a little dirty. Now I see with every movement how

I *own* him. I was a fool to think he would step out on me. He wants this. After long minutes he's sitting on, propped on his elbows, his whole magnificently muscled body gone rigid and tight, and as always he tugs at me a little. Always a gentleman, my Victor, trying to stop me before he finishes in my mouth. I don't let him. I take it and swallow it and make him mine again, and then he's pulling me up by the arms to kiss him and has me pinned down and I take him inside me again. A push on his chest and I'm on top, riding him.

During the night I lose count of how many times we fuck, making up for lost time. Three or four, at least. By morning I'm stiff and sore but I don't care. The warm water in the shower relieves the ache, even with him in there with me. I stand in the hot water wrapped in his arms, feeling the heat soak into my hair, the steam warm my joints. The ice queen has melted, and she's a puddle in his arms. I pray silently. Never take him away from me again. Never ever, please. I want to ride in his car. I want to go *home*.

It's nearly eleven when Alicia starts banging on the door. Check out time.

I open it for her.

"Did you two talk?" she asks.

"A little," I say, with a smirk.

She looks at me like I've sprouted another head.

"What now?"

"Go home. I'm riding with Victor."

Alicia nods, and heads back to her van. I need to make sure I pay her back for lunch yesterday. I'm *hungry*.

"Vic, I need food."

He sidles up behind me, kisses my cheek and gives my butt a light smack and a squeeze. Ordinarily I'd protest but I don't care anymore, let him show everyone. It doesn't matter.

"Pancakes," I say.

"IHOP," he says. "I know where there's a good one down here. I think," he says, sadly. "It's been a while."

The cleaning woman is on her way down the row by the time we finally leave. There's a spring in my step there hasn't been for years. I hop in the car eagerly, Vic starts her up and we ride to get some pancakes in his Firebird.

Whatever may come now, at least I had last night.

He yawns, and his expression darkens. There's a stop sign coming up.

"Eve?" he says. "The brakes aren't working."

Chapter Nineteen

Victor

When I touch the brake pedal nothing happens.

Well. That's not good.

"Eve," I say, trying not to panic. "The brakes aren't working."

"What?"

"The brakes. Are not. Working. Seat belt."

She pulls her seat belt on and grips the sides of the seat. I can't focus on her now. I need to stop the car. First thing, I start slowing her down using the engine as a brake. Shift down, use the engine's speed to slow the wheels. It's hard on the engine but I'd rather be hard on the engine than a greasy stain on the curb. I weave from side to side to bleed off inertia as I put her into neutral. The emergency brake does nothing. I think the lines have been cut. That stop sign is coming up awfully fast, and there's an oil truck headed the other way, ready to cross in front of me. The fucker is slowing down. If I don't stop

314

the car he'll smash right into us. Eve never makes a sound.

I weave across the road. The maneuver bleeds off some energy, and when the tires hit the soft shoulder, it draws off yet more. I nose over to the other side. If I try to use the shoulder to stop while we're going too fast, I'll lose control, maybe flip the car over.

Oil truck. Oil truck. Imminent oil truck.

I'm going slow enough to try it. I whip left, then right, into the dirt. The front wheel bites and throws up a plume of dust. I frantically pump the brakes, hoping against hope that the might give me a little traction.

The oil truck blows his horn and the world slows, dragging to a crawl. Now Eve screams, at last. It sounds like she screams for a million years, and the tires join her. The oil truck is on his brakes, but it's no use. He can't push too hard, or he'll turn, jacknife and flip over. The stop sign enters my peripheral vision and slides away, in a red flash. I'm looking through Eve's side of the car, through her window, and seeing a lot of grill and a shocked oil truck driver. Please, God, not like this.

Then, the oil truck is past and my windshield is full of corn. The car bounces, jounces, skids to a stop amid dead brown stalks, each a couple of feet high. The Firebird lurches and groans, shifts a bit, and finally stops.

Eve sits next to me wide eyed, clutching her chest. I grab her arm.

"Eve!"

She shrieks in alarm and throws herself at me. I stumble out of the car and around to her side, grab her and pull her to my chest. It feels like her heart is going to explode through mine. She takes quick breaths and I'm afraid she's going to start hyperventilating. Jesus. I pull Eve closer and stroke her hair, smooth it to her head. I hear shouting and here comes the oil man in his coveralls, yelling.

"What the hell are you doing?"

"My brakes failed," I shout back.

He stumbles to a stop. "No shit. How'd that happen?"

"I don't know."

"Is she okay?"

"Yeah," Eve manages.

"I'm going to take a look."

"Careful now," the oil man says.

I crouch down. I'm not going to try crawling under a car with no brakes and no way to chock the wheels, but it doesn't take much looking. The master cylinder has been sabotaged. Somebody punched a hole clean through it. I rock back on my heels and stand up, my head throbbing.

"What is it?" says Eve.

"Hole in the master cylinder. It gave me pressure long enough to drive down here, then gave out when the last of the fluid leaked out. I have no way to tell when it was done, damn it."

Oil truck me scratches his head. "Ya'll need a ride?"

"No, thanks."

"I should call the police, then," he says.

Oh. Shit. I'm on parole, I'm not supposed to leave the fucking state, except on business. Great.

"No," I say, quickly. "Thanks, we've got this. Right, Eve?"

She already has her phone out. Calling her assistant, I think.

I grin. Oil man hesitates, eyeing me. Please, just leave. Finally he turns.

"Okay then. Hell of a thing. I guess you're just lucky, then. Freak accident."

He turns and walks back up to his oil truck, gets inside, and drives off. It snorts diesel exhaust as it rolls away into the distance. I turn back to Eve.

"Yeah," she says, reading the sign into the phone. "Hurry. I know, I'm sorry."

She hangs up, and huffs.

"My assistant is coming."

"Good. Just pray a cop doesn't roll up. I'm not supposed to be here. A parole violation would ruin my day."

"Oh. Great."

I shrug.

Half an hour later, we're sitting on the Firebird's bumper and her assistant rolls up in a fucking Plymouth Voyager, I shit you not. At this point, I don't care. It could be a goddamn Volkswagen Beetle, as long as I can get out of here. Eve makes arrangements for a tow.

I look back at my car. My Dad's car.

Now it's personal, motherfucker.

I crawl into the back of the van. Eve gets in with me, instead of riding up front, and settles against me, her arm around mine.

"Hey now," her assistant says.

Eve snorts. "Alicia, this is Victor."

"Hello," she says, peering at me in the mirror. "I've heard a lot about you."

"It's all lies."

She smirks. "I hope not. Guess I have to ride you all back up home, huh?"

"Yeah," Eve yawns.

"I want pancakes."

They both glare at me.

"What happened?" Alicia asks.

"Somebody punctured the master cylinder on my car. They wanted to catch me off guard. Make it look like the brakes failed."

"You're sure somebody did that on purpose?"

I nod. "Had to be. It's a one in a million shot to..." I trail off.

"Victor?" Eve says, rising as I sit up next to her. She waits, biting her lip.

"My father died in a car accident," I say, calmly. "His brakes failed and a milk truck from a dairy farm up the road hit him at an intersection."

The whole car is quiet for a while.

"Victor," Eve says, very softly. "Did I ever tell you what happened to my mother?"

"No. I never asked. I didn't want to… I thought it would be painful."

Eve stares at nothing and murmurs, "A car accident."

I lean forward, fold my hands in my lap, and stare down at the floor. Fury burns in my lungs like hot smoke. I scrub my hands through my hair.

"I need access to Amsel's personnel files. You can do that, Eve."

"Yes. I just need a computer."

She chews her lip. She always does that when she's thinking, or upset. It's cute. I pull her close to me and she starts shaking. She was in that trough between the adrenaline release and the crash, and now it's hitting her hard. She squeezes me back, her eyes shockingly wide. Her assistant keeps eyeing me in the rear view mirror.

"Are we going back to the house? I'd like to go home today. I haven't seen my family in over twenty-four hours."

"We might be in a lot of trouble," I say, calmly. "I think we should stay away from the estate."

"Come with me, then," she says, without missing a beat.

I shrug. Eve doesn't protest.

Her eyes close, and she sleeps on my shoulder. She didn't get much sleep last night, that's for sure. After a rush like that, it's natural to crash out. It hits me, too. After a few minutes of violent shaking as that *I almost died* realization settles in, I start nodding off along with her. The next time I open my eyes, Eve is still asleep, it's mid afternoon and we're caught in traffic. In the suburbs. This Alicia must live a ways away from the estate, closer to the city. I've never been overly fond of this place. It's got all the crowding and congestion and stale air of the city and exactly none of the personality. It feels like a ten minute drive takes about two hours, and then we're pulling into a driveway in front of a cookie cutter house in a newly minted subdivsion that wasn't here when I went away.

Eve stirs, holds my hand as we step out and stretch. Her assistant leads us inside.

Then the kids show up. They must be four and five, a boy and girl, tending towards chubby like their mother.

"These are my kids," Alicia says, hesitantly. "Hunter and Ashley."

The kids seem fascinated by Eve. They crowd around her.

"Are you mom's boss?" the boy asks.

"Um," Eve says, visibly nervous. Kids always rattled her nerves. "Yes."

"Shoo, kids, mommy has work to do." She turns to us. "I have a home office. We can access the personnel files from there."

The home office turns out to be an unused third bedroom, half packed with school supplies and kid desks. Eve locks us in and Alicia sits down to bring up the corporate VPN, and switches seats so Eve could log in. I stand behind her as she waits for it to connect.

"What are we looking for?"

"Pull up your father's personnel file."

It takes her a minute to find it.

Of course, it's blank. No commendations, no write ups, no notes, no evaluations, nothing. Fortunately that's not what I'm looking for.

"Nothing here," Eve notes.

"Everything is here," I say, pointing to the screen with my finger. "Look. He came on board when I was..." I do some quick math in my head. "Nine."

"So?"

"So, my father died in a car accident when I was twelve."

Eve's voice goes cold. "Vic, not everything bad in your life ties back to my father."

"Your mom died in a car accident. What kind of car accident?"

"I don't..." she trails off. "We never spoke about it. If I asked he'd give me a few sentences, and if I bothered him..."

My hands rest on her shoulders. I can feel her shudder all the way up my arms. I squeeze, gently. She takes a deep breath. I can't help myself and start playing with her hair. Annoyed, she tugs at my hand, but not very hard.

"That doesn't mean much by itself," Alicia says.

"Does he have a private office?" I ask. I leave out *in my house*.

"Yes, back at our house in Philadelphia. He never sold it. He lives there most of the time, now."

I turn to Alicia. "Do you know where he is right now?"

"I'm not his assistant, but he's going to some kind of a function tonight. He won't be in town."

"Okay," I announce. "Just a little breaking and entering."

Eve shrugs her shoulders under my hands. "I have a key."

"Oh. Not so much the breaking, then. Just the entering."

Eve giggles.

"Have you two eaten today?"

Eve starts snickering to herself. I can't help it, I laugh a little, too.

"I'm serious. Kitchen. Now."

There's a command in her tone that I can't ignore, for some reason. The two of us end up in her little kitchen, eating fresh pancakes while her kids watch cartoons in the next room over. They seem a little young to be on their own. Maybe half an hour later their father rolls up, and is startled to see Eve in the kitchen when he walks in. He doesn't seem to know what to make of me. Alicia takes him aside to talk with him privately, away from us and the kids. I step away to make a phone call about my car. I have the towing company load her on a wrecker and bring her up to a garage I know that works on old General Motors cars. I'd do the repairs myself, but I don't think I'm going to find the time in the next few hours. Once that's done I sit at the table and feed Eve bites of pancake from my plate while she almost sits in my lap. We're like teenagers again.

No matter what happens, at least I have this, right now.

It gets late faster than I'd like. I really don't want Eve's poor assistant tied up in this, so I ask her to drive us to a rent-a-car place where I pick up a nondescript Hyundai and we drive into the city. Eve's old place isn't actually all that far from mine, maybe a twenty minute walk, but a much nicer part of the city, all ancient row houses, big Victorians. True to her word, Eve has a key and we walk right in the front door. She locks it behind us and I lead the way, slowly. There's no security system, or anything like that, but we leave the lights off anyway. It'll be dark soon, and it's already dark in the house. As I walk around, it strikes me how sterile everything is. This looks like one of those tour houses, where they invited people to walk through and gawk at old lamps. From the way Eve navigates the house, I'd say nothing has changed since she was a kid. She takes me around the corner from the entrance to a large room that takes up a whole corner of the house.

It reminds me, vaguely, of my father's study, except the antiques are all fake. It takes a practiced eye, or growing up in a three hundred year old house, to pick up on these things. No computer, at least none sitting out.

"I was never really allowed in here," Eve whispers.

I don't know why she's whispering, but I can see the fear making her tremble.

"What are we looking for?"

I shrug and start pulling at his drawers. Everything inside is inhumanly neat, like something out of an office supply catalog. Drawer after drawer.

The bottom one is fake, sort of. There's a safe bolted into the drawer itself. I crouch down, poke at it. I have no clue what the combination might be. Damn it.

Eve taps my shoulder.

"Look."

She's pulled a scrapbook down from one of the shelves. She starts flipping through it.

Newspaper clippings?

I'm a little surprised to see anyone keeps stuff like this anymore. Eve whips through the pages in a flurry, skimming the articles glued to the pages. Finally she stops.

"This one is about my mother," she says, calmly. "Here's her picture."

From the look on her face I can see she hasn't seen many photographs of her mother.

"Police said it was a freak accident," she says. Her voice tightens. "Her brakes failed and she hit a tree."

"Her brakes," I say.

"Jesus Christ," Eve murmurs.

It startles me. She's usually so proper in her speech, at least when we're not, ah, *in flagrante dilecto*.

"Do you think…"

"That your father murdered your mother, then my father, and then tried to kill me, or *us*, the same way? Yeah, I do."

"These articles don't make any sense," she says, sitting in a side chair to go over them. "I mean, the *articles* make sense but they're randomly chosen. They're from the business section, obituaries, there's an article here about a missing person…" she trails off.

"It's not a scrapbook," I say, softly. "It's a trophy case."

She looks up. "What? Oh my God, what?"

I swallow. "Eve, I think we better get out of here. Bring that."

She nods and tucks it under her arm.

A shadow passes by the window. I grab Eve and pull her down to her knees with me, and creep along the floor. I can feel her heart hammering against me and she presses into my side. Just someone walking outside, I think. Then I hear the front door open and freeze.

Whispers pass back and forth. I can't understand them.

Oh, they're loud enough, but they're in Russian.

I look at Eve. She looks at me. I motion for her to wait, and she goes stock still. I listen to the creak of feet on old floorboards. Three shadows, three men. I edge closer to the hallway, ready to spring.

All at once there's a gun in my face, a sleek black automatic with along cylindrical suppressor.

"Stand up," the gunman says, in lightly accented English. He's wearing a ski mask, as are his two friends. One of them aims at Eve.

I put my hands up and stand.

"Put the book on the desk," the other one says, indicating with his gun.

Eve rests the scrapbook on the desk and puts her hands up.

"Very good. You are coming with us now. Quietly."

One walks in front and holds the door while the other two walk behind. I can practically feel the guns pointed at my back. There's a nondescript gray van sitting out front, idling on the street. If somebody would just look they'd see three men with very illegal guns leading us outside, but in cities people have a way of not seeing, if there's anybody to see at all. The street looks deserted. They push Eve in first, then me. I sit next to her and two gunmen sit a cross from us, pistols resting on their laps, ready to shoot us. The third drives.

"So," I say. "Your place, or mine?"

"Shut up."

Turns out they're going to my place. I don't mean the apartment. I know as soon as I realize the route we're taking.

They're taking us back to the estate.

Chapter Twenty

Evelyn

Oh God, oh God, Oh God.

Victor doesn't move. His face is a frozen mask. I know my own is just as still, but I'm losing my mind. Please, not now. Don't let me have so short a time with him and take him away again. I press against him as much as I can.

I don't remember the ride back to the estate being so short. It feels like five hours. It feels like five minutes. When the van doors open into the dark and they push me out I stumble up the front steps, along with Victor, and into the house.

My father is sitting in a side chair in the foyer, as still as a statue. He might as well be cut from marble. Seated across from him, smoking a cigar, is a massive slab of a man, bald but with hairy hands and thick sausage fingers. Every one has at least one ring, and he's wearing gold chains around his neck. Big, ostentatious ones. From the description that Victor gave me, he can only be this Vitali person. He looks at me with something his eyes that makes me shiver. I feel like I'm being undressed. His expression goes flat when my father turns and looks at him over steepled fingers.

"There you are," Father says, in his usual expressionless tone.

"Hello, Martin," Victor says, his voice edged with malice.

"You," Father says. "You don't know how to behave, do you?"

"Out," says Vitali.

His three men leave, but Vitali pulls out a gun and rests it on his thigh.

"Do not be getting any ideas, boy."

"What's going on here?" Victor demands. He looks from one to the other. "What the hell?"

"You've been played," Vitali chuckles.

"I was willing to let this farce continue. Now it must come to an end. This is your fault, Eve. I want you to understand that."

I swallow.

"What is?"

"If you'd done as you were told, I'd have been willing to let you run off with him, until he was dealt with. Now you go behind my back, and force my hand."

"You two are working together?" Victor says, incredulous.

"No," Father says. "Vitali works for me."

There's something wrong with his voice. Father's diction and enunciation were always so perfect, so practiced. He sounds like a voice coach when he speaks, but his voice... slips.

He says something to Vitali in Russian and they both start laughing. When he switches back to English, he has an accent.

"You," he looks at Victor. "You are no end of trouble. So unpredictable. I should have known giving you two any time alone was a mistake, yes. I cannot have you two going behind our backs, trying to stop me. I had planned a more sophisticated means to deal with our problem, but you force my hand and brute force will have to do."

I feel my legs shaking, trying to collapse under me.

"The problem is this. When Karen died, everything passed to you, as per her will, as Victor had been disinherited. Somehow she grew..." his eyes roll as he searches for the word, "Disenchanted with me and decided she would rather pass all the Amsel holdings to you. Necessitating that I waste years of time working through you. I had hoped to make better use of you. Perhaps even come to trust you, but like your whore mother you are useless and must be gotten rid of."

"What?" I blurt out.

"You've pieced it together by now, I'm sure. Yes, I killed your mother. Not with my own hands, of course. I always have clean hands. I tried to teach you that, but you never learned. So long I tried to teach you, and you picked up all the wrong lessons," he shoots Victor a scathing glance. "You. I keep trying to turn you into an asset but you become a thorn in my side. I can't have you exposing me or interfering anymore. If you'd cooperated I'd have let you have her. She'd no longer have been any use to me. Truth is, some sentimentality leads me to prefer not to dispose of my only blood, but practicality must overrule sentimentality. You both have to die. With you gone there will be no one to contest my daughter's last will and testament or my status as her sole beneficiary."

"You think you can just get away with killing your own daughter?"

"No," he sighs. "You will. Or rather, you will commit murder suicide. You see, you were released from prison and began stalking and harassing her. I have evidence of this, of course. Once it was clear she'd moved on and rejected you, you lost your mind. Unable to cope, you broke in here, killed her, and set the house on fire."

"Tragic," Vitali adds, chuckling.

"I wait an appropriate time, of course, and after the necessary legal wrangling everything that belongs to your family is now mine."

"Why?" Victor says. "What did we ever do to you?"

Vitali starts laughing.

Father... *Martin* doesn't.

"You're expecting me to deliver, what is it, a monologue, yes? I suppose I should tie you up over a shark tank and reveal my entire dastardly plan to take revenge on your family for some slight. No. You were an easy target. This is business. Sentimentality is for idiots."

"You," Victor barks, looking at Vitali. "He sent you to prison."

"I make mistake. I do time. I get out. That is how game is played. Sorry boy. You were right not to trust me. Whoever said not to make friends inside, give good advice."

"Let's go," Martin says, standing.

Vitali steps behind us, covering our backs with his gun. Martin keeps his distance, and leads us upstairs, to Victor's father's office. It still smells the same inside, the air stale from remaining closed up so long. I catch a whiff of a bitter, sulfurous smell and wrinkle my nose.

"That's gas," Victor says, softly.

Vitali's men are carrying jerry cans through the house, slopping it everywhere. They throw it on the walls, soak it into the carpet, pour it down the bannisters. The smell is overpowering.

In the office, they take Victor and shove him down into his father's chair. Vitali takes a heavy rope while Martin holds the gun on us, and winds it around Victor's arms.

"They'll know he was tied up," I point out.

"They will, but *they* will support my narrative, just like *they* would have convicted Victor no matter what he said or his lawyers did. Money is power, Eve. I tried to teach you that, but you keep forgetting your lessons. If you'd been more tractable and cooperative, I wouldn't have to get rid of you. It's a pity."

He didn't feel anything for me. I could see it. He was looking at me like I was a potted plant.

All those times he punished me, *hurt me*, he didn't *care*. Somehow that makes it worse. It must have been like whipping a dog that pissed on the carpet. I feel cold, all through my body, like my blood is freezing in my veins.

"Still, I'm not cruel. I'm not going to let you burn alive."

He turns. He's going to shoot me in the head instead.

While he's not quite facing me, I lunge at him. Caught off guard, he cries out in surprise. I rake my nails down his cheek, and go for his eyes.

"Get her off me!" he bellows.

Vitali grabs at me. I get my mouth on the meat of his hand and *bite*. He howls in pain, and punches me in the stomach. All the wind goes out of my lungs, and I double over in agony and collapse to the floor.

The big desk turns up with a massive grunt from Victor, topples, and he throws himself at Vitali. Martin, clutching his bleeding face in one hand, searches the room for the gun. He dropped it when I attacked him. He spots it. So do I.

I leap for it, feel my fingers on the grip. He tromps on my hand and I scream, try to pull out from under his hand, but he grinds his heel and twists his foot. I think I can feel bones breaking. It's like he's going to rip my hand right off. He bends, reaches for the gun.

Vitali crashes into him. Somehow, Victor got the ropes off and has the thick cord looped around Vitali's neck. He's clawing at it, turning purple, lying on top of Martin in a heap. Victor has his knee in Vitali's back, pulling the rope in both hands, twisting it like he means to saw through the man's neck. Father's fingers graze the grip of the dropped pistol and he tries to pull it towards him.

A letter opener glints on the carpet. I snatch it, raise it high and bring it down. The blade punches through the back of Father's hand and into the floor with a solid *thump* and he bellows in agony, trying to claw it loose.

I grab the gun, roll away. Victor pulls aside.

Martin pulls his hand loose and rolls, just as I pull the trigger. The report rings in my ears, and the gun jumps in my hand. My shot went wild, blew a hole in some books on the shelves. Father is on me before I can aim at him again. He collapses on top of me, pinning my arms to the side, grabs my wrist and squeezes so hard it feels like he'll put his thumb through the bones. I scream in agony and the gun drops from my limp hand. A savage backhand knocks me away, the world flashing white as his knuckles hit my jaw, and the room tilts and spin when my head hits the edge of a bookcase. My head is wet, and my hand comes away slick. I try to get up but I can't. Vitali rolls on top of Victor and Martin aims the gun at him.

Victor lets go, holds his hands apart in surrender.

Vitali pulls the rope loose and clambers up on all fours, gasping and rasping.

"Idiot," Martin barks, and shoots him.

It comes so fast I don't know how to process it. There's a flash and a bang and a wad of Vitali's head meat hits the books with a loud *slap* that I can somehow hear despite the gunshot. He flops down limp, and Martin aims the gun at Victor.

Then swings it over to me.

"I changed my mind. I will let you burn to death, you annoying little cunt. Make one move, Amsel, and I'll put a bullet in her hip. Bad way to die."

He backs through the door, and slams it closed. Victor is on his feet in an instant, smeared in blood from the huge dead Russian. He shoves the door open but it pushes back, and then there's a loud *whump* and flames so hot they're almost clear lick up under the door.

"They put gas on the fucking door," Victor bellows.

He rushes to my side and cradles my head in his hand. "Eve, Jesus, you're bleeding."

More *whumps* outside, and the sound of glass breaking.

I start to get up. "We have to get out of here."

He nods, rushes up the ladder to the second level, to the door to the cupola. He throws his full weight against it, over and over, screaming each time.

"It's boarded up or something. I can't get it open."

My head is bleeding. I clutch my hand to my scalp, trying to stop it. My other hand is throbbing, already swelling up. I think he broke something. There's more smoke coming in, rising under the door like vengeful spirits, swirling. It's starting to darken the air in the room. I cough.

"Victor, get down here," I call out, "Smoke rises."

"If we don't get out of here, we're both dead."

He throws himself at the door again.

There's something odd. The smoke is swirling, gathering around one of the bookcases. I blink a few times, trying to understand what I'm seeing. It's flowing between the cracks between the bookcase frames, and there's a little swirl like a whirlpool around the hole in the book from my wild shot.

"Victor! Get down here!"

"Damn it, I've almost got the door-"

"Victor, I think I found a way out."

He looks over the railing and rushes down, sliding down the ladder. He stops next to me and stares, as I start coughing.

"Get down," he says, almost pushing me to the floor. I breathe a little easier, take a deep breath. Victor sees it, too. He shoves his finger in the bullethole, then rips the book of the shelf, then more.

"Help me," he says.

I lurch to my feet. With my blood-slick hand, I start wrenching books off the shelf, one after another after another, and pile them on the floor. Finally there's only one left on the shelf. It doesn't budge when I pull at it.

"What the hell?"

"The underground fucking railroad," Victor almost cheers. "Get ready. We have to run. When I open the door the air is going to feed the fire, it might get through the door. Wait."

He runs to the other side of the room, yanks his father's chair from the floor and smashes open the glass gun cabinet. He pulls out an old double barrel and a box of shells, and tosses another to me. I catch it against my chest. He yanks on the stuck book and it comes loose with a *pop* and a *thunk* behind the shelf. It falls open, and there is a solid *boom* behind us. Victor pushes me inside as the flames road around the door, just *eat it*, the sides folding in and turning to ash as the fire reaches through, hammering the wood with a burning fist. Victor slams the door shut behind us and braces his shoulder into it as the office lights up like a sunrise, flames rushing up the wall and flowering over the ceiling. It's almost beautiful. The shock batters at the door and he coughs, hacks, coughs again.

We're in some kind of tunnel. The stones are old, part of the structure of the house itself, but they're getting hot and smoke is pouring in from the false bookcase door. Victor seizes my arm and almost holds me up as we run. The tunnel only goes a few feet to a tight spiral staircase that twists down through what must be one of the big columns outside. I stumble my way down, almost knocking him over when I hit the bottom. Victor pulls me along and we stoop through a narrow, low tunnel barely tall enough to stand in. I don't know where it goes but I can feel the heat from the flames above. There's a great crack and behind us stones and dust fall into the tunnel. The staircase folds with a loud groan, and we're trapped. The only way out is through. Victor grabs my hand and pulls me along. My hand throbs but I don't care.

The tunnel goes on, and on, and on. Finally there's an end, but it's just dirt. A horrid wave of panic hits me as I realize we're trapped, we've just run from a fiery death into a grave. It might be ten feet of dirt over our heads, ready to collapse. Then Victor slams the butt of the shotgun against something over his head and there's a sound of wood groaning and shearing and a sudden rush of cool, sweet air. Then Victor is lifting me up and I sit on the edge of a square cut stone pit and roll over the side, just as he pulls himself up beside me. He looks behind me, a look of naked agony on his face.

The house is burning. Flames lick up through the windows, pour out of the chimneys. The fiery tongues slice the ivy away in burning, charred strands. There is a *crack* and one of the columns holding up the roof over the terrace gives from the heat, and the whole thing folds and noses in.

Victor just stares, the flames painting his face a bruised color, shining in his eyes.

I shake his arm. "What do we do?"

"Shit. I don't know. Where the fuck is Martin?"

"I don't know. Where are we?"

"There's another… you gotta be fucking kidding me," he blurts out. "Follow me. I'm not leaving you here."

"Where are we going?"

"There's another tunnel."

Chapter Twenty-One

Victor

"We're leaving," I tell her, and take her into the Scary Tunnel.

Eve never says a word, she just follows me, clutching my hand with hers. Her skin is sticky, dried blood from her scalp. It's not as bad as she probably thinks it is. Any scalp wound bleeds like a stuck pig. It's matted in her hair, a dark clump of rust on the white gold.

She keeps her head down as we traverse the tunnel. My every step is sure. I know where I'm going. The first time I came through here, it felt five miles long. First thing I need to do is get Eve to safety, then I need to get my hands on Martin. The son of a bitch is not getting away with this. The end of the tunnel isn't far. Once we reach it I open the trap door and Eve hauls herself up the short staircase and out, and I'm right behind her, breathing free air on the other side of the wall.

"What is all this?"

"My family used to shelter runaway slaves," I tell her, panting. "Back during the Civil War. Before that, too, I guess."

I can see the flames over the treeline. It's all burning, everything.

"The house," she says.

"Fuck the house. Pictures of my Mom and Dad. Pictures of you and me. My life was in that house…" I trail off.

"No," I touch her shoulder and pull her to me. "My life is right here. The rest of it can be replaced. Let's get out of here, I want you safe."

"How?"

The Toyota is still parked under the trees. My neighbor the dairy farmer must not have noticed it. Please let the key still be in the ignition. Of course, it is. The door is still unlocked. I help Eve into the passenger's seat, rush around to the other side, and start her up. It's rough going back to the road.

Headlights flash in my rear view mirror. Oh shit.

I tromp the pedal and the little hatchback gives her all. I suddenly feel sorry for disparaging her before. I wish for the Firebird but the Firebird is sitting in a garage somewhere right when I need her. The Toyota tries her best, and I weave from one side of the road to the other, so they can't ram me, but there's headlights up ahead. I should have known. Martin wasn't going to just leave us to die without some kind of plan B. I don't think they figured on me, though. I weave around the oncoming truck, gripping the wheel so hard it creaks. The front tire hits soft shoulder but I wrestle the car back onto the road, a dazed Eve lurching this way and that in the seat behind me. Eve has the shotgun.

"You know how to load that?"

She shakes her head.

"Push the lever on the top. It opens in the middle. Stick the shells in the holes. They can only go in the one way. Don't touch the triggers."

As she fumbles with it, I drive. There's two packs of them hot on our tail, and they're catching up. The Toyota's little motor is screaming, but it's built light, to save weight for gas mileage. She holds her own, especially on these winding roads where the big lumbering trucks have to slow for turns. I don't. Eve snaps the gun closed.

There's a flash behind us. They say you never hear the one that gets you. That's because the bullet goes faster than the sound, and the crack comes after the back glass shatters. Something spins and bounces on my lap. They hit the rear view mirror, knocked it right off the mount and popped a hole in the windshield, a spiderweb folding across my vision. I weave in the road as they fire again, more flashes, more pops. The mirror on Eve's side shatters into a million pieces, and falls away into the night. Another crack and her window blows out.

"Get *down*," I bark at her, pushing her down into the footwell.

It doesn't matter. For bullets a car like this might as well be made of tinfoil. There's no cover from a bullet in here. I see a flash. Headlamps, this time.

A Mercedes. It's fucking Martin, weaving around the two trucks.

I can't outrun them, but I can't outdrive them. I can't outdrive Martin, not in that. Fucking German engineering.

I pull Eve back against the seat. She winces, clutching her hand.

"Seat belt!" I bellow, and she doesn't even blink before she yanks it on. I fumble at mine and take a sharp turn one-handed, the wheel straining against my wrist. I burned my hand somehow and I don't even realize it until now, when the wheel starts to slide in my palm and grinds against the burn, sending lancing agony up my arm.

Martin swings wide. He's trusting in the speed and handling of his machine. I can't slow down in a sharp turn, have to put more power to the drive wheel to keep from losing control. He might be overcorrecting, he might be doing it on purpose, but the end result is the same. The big Benz side-swipes the little Toyota and then we're bouncing and the cracked windshield is full of sky, then dirt. For a single gut-twisting moment I think we might roll but she stays upright, jounces down the hill into a dead field, crashing through more cut corn stalks. Fucking corn. Martin's Mercedes grinds to a stop and he surges out, gun in hand.

I draw the shotgun out of Eve's hands smoothly, in a single motion, but the seat belt catches my leg as I kick the door open and I go down. I squeeze one trigger. Martin is already down, but his driver's side door window shatters along with the shocking report of the shotgun. I have another shot. I roll, free my leg, touch off the other trigger, punch a dozen holes in Martin's door but he's not there. He was moving around the other side. Eve is out of the car. Moving around the front, crawling. Good girl. The engine block will give her some cover, the bullets will go through the car but not the solid aluminum block of the engine. There are some shells on the floor. The box I was carrying split open sometime, maybe during the crash, maybe before. I grab a handful, shove two down the shotgun's throat and get up.

At some point, I hurt my leg. Can't worry about that now. Martin is over there somewhere. I can't see him.

I guess if this was a movie, wind would blow, the soundtrack would come up, and we'd face off, staring each other down for a moment before firing the climactic shot of our duel. Instead,

Martin looks startled when he sees me and starts shooting wildly, and so do I.

Just like they said, I don't hear the one that gets me. I never hear the sound, just feel as sledghammer in my thigh. A second too late I tug both triggers and the shotgun goes off. I lurch around and Martin spins. I see blood. I think I got him.

He turns back and clutches his face. Somehow I missed with a fucking *shotgun*. He strides over, clutching his face. There's blood between his fingers. I got his ear. Hah.

I clutch my leg. That's a lot of blood. It doesn't hurt.

I'm pretty sure that's bad. I'm sorry, Eve.

Martin kicks the shotgun away, not that I could have reloaded it. He raises the pistol and aims at my head.

"Boy, you are no end of trouble. It will be very difficult to explain this."

"Yeah," I manage to rasp, "Sorry about that."

He shrugs, and then Eve picks up the shotgun and swings it like Ol' Betsy in a cheap Western and bashes the buttstock right into Martin's skull. His hands shock open and the pistol drops right out of his grip. He turns back, moves to grapple the gun away from Eve, but she recovers from the swing and puts her full weight into it, twisting it like she's swinging a baseball bat. The stock hits his upper arm and there's a solid meaty *crack*, and he howls, clutching at the limb. Her backswing catches him right on the kneecap.

Watching a man's leg fold up the wrong way is unpleasant, even if it's a simple fuck like Martin Ross.

He goes down to the ground, rolls. His hand slips behind his back.

Of course fucking Martin would have a backup. He slips the little black pistol from his back pocket. Eve doesn't see it. She raises the shotgun over her head, ready to bring the sharp bottom corner of the buttstock right down on his fucking head, but I can already see it playing out, as in slow motion. He's going to shoot her right in the gut.

His pistol, the one he dropped, is slick with blood in my hand. Doesn't matter. I put the muzzle against the side of Martin's head. He stops as he feels it. Eve sees the pistol in his good hand.

Bang, bang. Once and then twice for sure. Eve screams. She's covered in blood.

Mostly not hers. That works for me.

The shotgun falls with a thump in the dry dirt and suddenly she's tugging at my arm.

I'm so tired. I need a nap. Just let me sleep, damn it.

When I don't get up she locks both arms around mine and pulls me over the ground. She wraps something around my leg and shoves me in the passenger's seat. I flop over as she pushes the door shut and climbs in the other side. The little Toyota groans as she pulls back up onto the road.

You know, I've never let her drive. I wasn't even sure she *could*. Guess it doesn't matter.

I fade in and out. Red and blue lights bruise the night sky. Eve stops the car, gets out screaming and waving her hands.

At some point, somebody picks me up. I keep calling for Eve.

A small, silky hand closes tight around mine.

"I'm here," she says, over and over and over. "I'm here."

I keep hearing it as I drift off.

When I finally wake up again I feel like I'm covered in concrete. The lights blind me, so I press my eyes shut. Eve's soft hand grips mine.

"Hey," she murmurs.

I still can't open my eyes.

"Where the hell am I?"

"You're in the hospital, Vic. You got shot in your leg and your hand was pretty badly burned."

"Oh."

That would explain why my leg hurts so badly I'd like to tear it off.

I finally manage to get my eyes open. Eve has a bandage around her head and a cast on her hand.

"It's not as bad as it looks," she says, quickly.

I touch her cheek. She rubs against my palm.

"They won't let me get in the bed with you, but they can't make me leave."

I listen patiently as she tells me what's going on. First, and most importantly, I'm not going back to prison. As soon as she was able, she sent Alicia and her lawyers to Martin's house, gathered up a mound of evidence linking him to, well, everything, and papers were being filed to plead for an official pardon from the governor. There was quite a bit of proof that I was not involved in anything I was convicted of.

It's a shame Martin died. Apparently head wounds like that are fatal. If he was alive he'd be under in investigation for murder. For Evelyn's mother, for my father, for *my* mother; the police were looking into the possibility of poison. For all of them and for Brittany Andrews.

Martin wasn't big on loose ends. Brittany bought a new car with her generous severance package after my trial, and moved to Arizona. A few weeks later her steering gave out and she crashed into a ditch. She wasn't found out there for over a week. Crash wasn't fatal.

Suddenly all my anger at her tastes bitter and cruel and I try to will it away, but I can't stop myself from knowing I felt it, if that makes any sense.

After a long discussion, Eve and I decided to take Amsel public. As the sole owner she had the right. The company was in rough shape and the initial public offering was dicey. It cut her net worth by two-thirds, but it brought legitimate investors on board and Eve retained a large interest in the company, enough to turn things around. Good people there could bring some honor back to the family name, I guess. I was done with that, and so was she. The dividends from her stock go in the bank, and she took out a hefty chunk to help me follow my dreams and go along with me.

There was nothing to do about the house. By the time I was ready to limp my way out to see it, there was nothing but a burnt, charred shell, a few piles of bricks here and there sticking up like the carcass of a long dead animal, baked in the sun. It's amazing the kind of things that survive a fire. A photo album came out, almost untouched, and my father's magnifying glass, a few things here and there. In one wing of the house there was an antique chair just sitting there with some black soot on the seat. I don't even know how to explain that. What could be salvaged, was salvaged. We sold off the land to a developer and banked the money, not needing all that much. There was an insurance claim, of course. Since Martin and Vitali set the fire, we cashed in big time. My parents and so on back through the generations were meticulous about inventorying the contents of the house, and those antiques inside were probably worth more than the land. The insurance hadn't been updated since Dad died, but it was more than enough to set us up for life.

I had everything I needed. The garage, not being attached to the house, survive the fire. We sold all the cars.

Except one, obviously. She was waiting for me at the garage where I had the truck tow her. It was like the scene at the end of the movie where the hero's dog has miraculously survived and runs up before they all head into the sunset. Except the car just sat there, being a car. I mean, I was conceived in the back seat of that thing, I'm pretty sure. It was my dad's car, and now it's all that's left of him. Other than me, I mean. Eight generations of Amsel men fought in the Revolution and the Civil War, built a huge financial empire, built that house. Now all that remains is me and my Trans-Am.

We could do lots of things, the two of us. Start a new business, buy into others, find work in the financial sector, become angel investors.

After I spend two days repairing the Firebird and find a body shop to fix up the paint scratches from the corn, Eve looks at me.

"Let's open our own shop."

Far be it from me to argue with her.

Chapter Twenty-Two

Evelyn

It took me a while to get used to the smell of motor oil, but here I am.

Carlisle, Pennsylvania is the last place I expected to end up. If you told me years ago I'd be sitting in a cramped office above a garage while my husband works under a '68 Chevelle replacing the transmission, doing the books for his garage, I'd have laughed in your face. Yet here I am. This is child's play compared to the kind of work I'm used to, mostly arithmetic. I should have known. We've been at it two years now and the Amsel Motors has gained a nationwide reputation for restorations of vintage General Motors automobiles. Just last week I oversaw taking out a loan to install a second rotisserie- not for cooking, a big machine that lifts cars and spins them around effortlessly, turning them all around for the restoration work. Victor can tell the year and model of just about any car with a glance at the headlights and I've seen him turn rusted out hulks into gleaming, beautiful works of art. Not least his Dad's Firebird, his first project. It has pride of place out front, gleaming black and menacing in front of the office. The new paint job is incredible.

I'm done, ready to close the books. I take a certain enjoyment from doing it old school, keeping track of everything on paper. Everything around here is like that, mechanical, simple. It brings a certain comfort to our surroundings. The only computer in the shop is in the corner of the office here. I use it to process orders for parts when Vic sends them up. I glance up at the clock, and see it's an hour past quitting time.

Sure enough, when I descend the staircase, Victor is still under the car he's working on, tinkering.

"Honey," I say, planting my fist on my hips. "It's quitting time. Come on."

Sighing, he ducks out from under the car. He is, of course, covered in grease.

"Let me get cleaned up."

"I'll go get started on dinner. If you don't show up in fifteen minutes I'm coming back to get you."

He gives me that look and heads off to clean up as I walk outside and across the long gravel drive to the house. We bought a manufactured house; it came in big sections on trucks and they put it together for us. For the first year we lived in the cramped apartment above the garage, which now serves as a storage room. Inside, I want to collapse into a chair but instead I put a pot of water to boil for macaroni and cheese and toss a pack of hot dogs in a pan to heat up. Simple fare, but as long as we're eating together it works for me.

Victor comes in after exactly fourteen minutes. *Cleaning up* means de-greasing himself. He kisses me on the cheek and ducks into the bathroom, and the shower starts. A half an hour later he comes out clean, and dinner is ready. There's still a faint smell of oil about him, as there always is, but I've started to like it. We serve ourselves, bumping into each other purposely at the stove, and sit down in front of the television. Victor wears a thin t-shirt, and his tattoos show through.

I lean on the arm of the sofa while I eat, with my legs over his. He twists off the cap of his beer, then mine, and our fingers brush when he passes it to me. I scarf down my food in big bites, barely chewing. Vic eats and swigs from his beer, and I drink mine down in big gulps. Before we moved in here I'd never even had a beer- when we dared out eat back during our college days I never drank, and I would occasionally take wine at the stupid parties my father made me attend while I was working for him, but only because I had to. I've learned to love the hoppy, bitter taste of the brews Vic picks out. He's a beer snob.

Our plates end up on the coffee table, beside a few empty beers for each of us. I'm feeling tipsy, and daring.

So, I slip onto his lap. He snatches the remote and turns off the TV, and his hand slip up under my t-shirt, and he pulls me into a kiss as I straddle him. My hands slide under his shirt. His skin is still damp from the shower, and so is his hair. I twirl a finger in it. He lets it hang to his shoulders now, in thick coal black curls. He starts to tug my shirt up, and I stand up, pulling his hands. Without a word, he follows me down the hall and almost pushes me onto the bed. I fall face down and he tugs my jeans down as I undo the button. Once they're over my hips and ass they slide right off, and my underwear comes next, then his warm mouth on the small of my back, working his way up to peel off my shirt and unhook my bra.

He gets on top of me and slides his hands up my back, kneading the muscle. I twist and wriggle out of my shirt, and my bra, and lay there naked, sighing into the bed as he massages my back. He runs his hands down my legs, and rubs my feet. I don't know how they end up so sore, but they do. It tickles a little and I can't help laughing. When I do, he smacks me lightly on the butt and I laugh harder and wriggle out from under him, then spring on him. It's his turn. I get his boxers down and he's already hard for me, but I press his erection against his stomach and rub my belly against it as he pulls his shirt over his head. I slide up, so he can feel the heat between my legs, and bury my face in his soft hair and breathe deep.

My trick, he calls it. I sit up and slide my sex along the length of his shaft, and the look on his face is priceless. He can't keep his hands off my breasts, my ass, my neck. He pulls me down and kisses me and rolls on top of me. Once he's on top he tickles my sides and grinds his cock against me, kisses me hard. I want him now and he knows it, so he holds back, kisses my throat, nips and suck at the soft skin, starts working his way down. I groan and roll my hips, urging him on, but he slows, stops, slowly kisses his way across my collarbone from one side to the other before he shoves his face in my armpit and sniffs. I try to push him down, but he struggles.

I'm still laughing at he takes my nipple in his mouth, slides his arms around me and sucks. My sex is throbbing, my thighs slick, but still he takes his time, making happy little noises as he sucks. Shivers pass through me, but not from cold. I push on his head and he finally relents, licking down my middle to dive between my legs and softly lick my slit. With a groan I spread my legs and let my arms fall limp on the bed, close my eyes and savor the sensations as he slowly works his way around, tonguing and teasing the skin of my inner thighs before he gives me another lick, each touch making my clit throb. Then his mouth as his finger slips inside, and I can't take it, I have to have him inside me.

He rises up, wipes his chin with his arm, slides on top of me and pushes his cock into my sex. I curl my fingers in his hair and savor the feeling of his shaft pushing into my walls, the feeling of my body swallowing him. Somehow I feel surrounded and enveloped as I take him inside me and he puts his arms around me and I dig my fingers into his back. He always fucks me harder when I scratch him, and tonight I want it hard. I'm celebrating. I urge him on with my legs, rake his back with my nails, moan and whimper and breathe in his ear, begging him to fuck me harder.

When he slows, he rolls and pulls me on top of him. I sit up and ride him hard, eyes closed, my nails digging into his chest as he holds my sides, steadies me as I ride. I could do this forever, but I'm so horny I can't make myself slow down and savor it anymore. Soon I'm quivering, my back rounded as I lean over him, and he's taken over again, thrusting into me from below. He pulls me to him, holds me close and digs his heels into the bed, driving into me. When I come he almost loses his grip on me, for my thrashing. It's so intense all I can do is bunch up and squeak, the waves of pleasure too intense to breathe. He holds me tight as he finishes, throbbing inside me.

I go limp on top of him, let him slip out of me and snuggle up to his side. This is going to be one of those nights, and I want him to rest before we go again.

"I have something I really need to tell you," I whisper.

"Yeah?"

"Victor. You're going to be a father."

He sits up, and I rise up on my elbows.

"The test was positive. The one I took on Monday. I went to the doctor yesterday morning and they called me with the results. I'm pregnant."

I'm not sure how he's going to react, but he whoops with joy, snatches me up off the bed and flops me down, so I'm lying with my head at the foot of the bed, and kisses me hard, holding me tight. I reach down between his legs and stroke him, and he growls in my ear.

Round two is going to start a little early.

Thank you for reading *Blackbird*. I hope you enjoyed it!

Comments are welcome at abbygrahamromance@gmail.com

For more information on current and upcoming books, please sign up for my newsletter here: eepurl.com/0qieT

Also by Abigail Graham

Serials

Paradise Falls

Book One: Scar Tissue

Book Two: Open Wounds

Book Three: Turning Point

Book Four: Spy Games

Book Five: Shock Waves

Novels

Blackbird

Thrall